FEEL FREE TO SCREAM

Copyright © 2022 Boris Bacic
All rights reserved.

Feel Free To Scream

"When the law fails to serve us, we must serve as the law."
- Kenneth Eade, Paladine

Feel Free To Scream

Contents

Prelude 7
First Blood 15
Anticipation 27
The News 35
Resolve 45
Curiosity 53
Apples 61
Swordmaster 71
Publicity 85
Copycat 99
Suburbs 111
The Letter 123
Interrogation 133
Culprit 141
Rush 149
Red Riding Hood 155
Portland Executioner 161
Final Notes 167
More from the author 169

Feel Free To Scream

1

PRELUDE

My first kill was an accident. I certainly hadn't imagined things going down that way when I drove three hours down I-5 in my crappy Dodge to visit my little sister's rapist in Medford. I hadn't even known what I planned on doing at the time. It wasn't like I had packed some rubber gloves, chloroform, and a gun with a silencer and drove down there with the clear intention to kill him.

No, what started out as a drive to clear my head ended up changing my entire life.

I was angry for the injustice Summer had suffered because of Robert. Summer was only twenty-two and Robert almost thirty when they started dating. The two of them were like unmatched socks, not only personalities-wise but also visually.

Summer was liked by everyone. Her innocent, cherub-like face, accompanied by the persistent grin of her lips and the high-pitched tone of her voice, which nearly sounded like it was sped up in an audio program, were enough to convince anyone within the first minute that she was the kindest soul ever to exist. In fact, I didn't think the word "hurt" or "evil" were even listed in her dictionary.

Our cousin Mark once called her Little Red Riding Hood. When we asked him why that name, he said, "Because you're as naïve as Little Red Riding Hood." The name kind of stuck whenever Mark was around. I liked it, but Summer didn't.

Robert, on the other hand, was the polar opposite of Summer. His greasy, wannabe rock star hairstyle, beard that grew in uneven patches, and faded, ugly-looking sleeve that looked like one of those temporary sticker tattoos you could buy at Walmart for a dollar all spelled trouble the moment we laid eyes on him.

Not that I'm judgmental of people who have tattoos. I think they're great. But you know how you can sometimes tell what kind of a person to expect just based on their clothing style or body art? Well, your first assumption about Robert would be that he wastes away in his mom's basement, smoking weed and drinking while listening to heavy metal—and you'd be right.

As soon as Summer introduced Robert to me and the parents, we made it our life's mission to break them apart at any cost. In fact, my family members weren't the only ones who saw the incongruity between Summer and Robert. When they walked down the street—her in a loose summer dress (no pun intended) that showed off her slim feature, and him with a broken cigarette in his mouth and slouching like an old scarecrow—people's gazes inadvertently fell on them.

It was like spotting a mascot on the street. It's usually a Marvel superhero like Spiderman, and you could see that the underpaid employee working part-time, trying to cheer up passersby, fit in the costume about as well as my ex in an XXL condom.

It wasn't difficult to imagine what the people looking at Summer and Robert were thinking. The guys wondered how such a punk managed to hook up with such a cute girl. The women would wonder why such an innocent-looking girl was dating someone who looked like he'd just come from a two-day-long Slipknot concert.

The problem with Summer, however, was that the more we told her not to do something, the more she leaned toward it. We could have told her she was too much of a pussy to jump out the window, and she would have done it without even opening the window just to prove us wrong—not that she ever did that.

Our parents had tried telling her that Robert wasn't a good fit for her, but they were too aggressive in their methods, and that only made Summer spite them more. It would have been comical had it not been so painful to watch.

Here she was, graduating to become a psychologist so she could help people resolve their problems, and then there was Robert, whose grandiose plan of earning money was investing in Bitcoin and other cryptocurrencies.

Come to think of it, one of the reasons why Summer started dating Robert in the first place must have been because she thought she could fix him.

That's how it always goes, right? We want to be a hero and help someone, and we end up fucking ourselves over because the saying is correct—you can't help someone who doesn't want to be helped.

Robert was the epitome of not wanting any help. He was okay where he was, content with the cold relationship he had with his mother and had no contact with his father, pretty much developing the level of empathy that could be compared to a sewer rat.

While Mom and Dad tried their hostile approach, I talked to Summer in a diplomatic way and explained to her with as much neutrality as I could muster that she needed to think about her own future. Somehow, she saw through my ruse, and our conversation ended with her telling me that nothing would ruin her and Robert's love before storming out.

But something did ruin their love, and it came very soon. That something was Robert himself. Summer and I lived together in an apartment in Portland, and it wasn't difficult to see when she wasn't herself, even after a whole day of working with pain-in-the-ass interviewees at my work.

It wasn't long before Summer started coming home downcast and sometimes outright tear-stricken. One tiny nudge was enough to get her to open up. The relationship with Robert was apparently going terribly.

She caught him chatting up other girls up online and sending them dick pics, only to give Summer a pathetic excuse that he was doing it so they would stop bothering him (I had the bad luck of seeing one of the pictures, and I could see why someone would stop bothering him after sending it.)

He had also eyed other girls while he and Summer were out in town and hadn't even bothered to hide it. According to Summer—and I have no reason to believe she lied—Robert would sometimes look at a girl, make a horny grimace, and grab at his crotch while exclaiming what a nice ass or pair of tits the girl had.

Summer's confrontation about it ended with him shifting the blame on her. It got to the point that she actually came close to believing it was okay for a boyfriend to behave like that in public because of his "manly urges."

Then there were other things that Summer couldn't really convey into words, but I saw some of them very clearly. Like how he forgot important dates even though Summer went above and beyond to make him happy for his birthday and their anniversary; how he went out with his friends and didn't answer any of her messages or calls for well over two days. He often made derisive comments, telling her she needed to lose weight because this or that dress looked bad on her. He had fits of jealousy when random guys would send her friend requests even though she never spoke to them, etc.

Duplicity at its best.

The thin drywall of their relationship had started cracking, but I still couldn't do anything to help Summer. Even the mention of the word "breakup" had her justifying Robert's actions and telling me I was wrong.

So instead, I decided to let her come to her own conclusions. I figured she wouldn't stay with Robert for long – no one could take such mistreatment forever, right? Plus, Summer had all these wooers online and in real life, and it was only a matter of time until someone gave her a compliment or two, and she would see that she deserved better than Robert.

That sounded like a good plan in my mind, and I was perfectly content with it. I didn't like seeing Summer suffering, but I knew that I had to be patient. And boy, did I have to be patient.

Exactly one year, three months, and five days after they had started dating, Summer finally broke up with Robert. I didn't think she had it in her, to be honest, so I was especially proud of my little sister.

She was heartbroken, of course, while I had to suppress the urge to celebrate. I gave her a shoulder to cry on and listened as she ranted about Robert, pretty much echoing all the bad stuff that we'd been telling her for the past year, three months, and five days.

It took her a while to get back on her feet, but after four months, Robert was only a distant memory. Summer had even started dating a nice guy named Matias, who worked as a data scientist at Zillow.

Robert had tried calling her from different unblocked numbers multiple times over the course of those four months, but she never answered.

One day, however, she faltered and accepted his call. He begged to see her in person, and she conceded. That's how it usually goes, right? If you stay in touch with your ex, you're bound to get back together sooner or later.

I was sure that Robert and Summer were going to get back together again and that this agony would get prolonged for another five or so years while they broke up and made up over and over.

I told her not to go. In fact, I pleaded with her. I had a really bad feeling about the whole thing, but Summer was still Summer, which meant she would do things her own way, and there was nothing that would convince her otherwise. I couldn't really accompany her. She was twenty-three already, and I had to give her the benefit of the doubt and trust her to act like a mature woman.

While she was gone, I spent the hour flicking between social media apps on my phone and mindlessly scrolling through the myriad videos of adorable puppies, desserts coated in so much chocolate they were guaranteed to cause diabetes, and wannabe fitness instructors who showed exercises for "healthy knees" as if they had just discovered fire.

When I heard the door opening, I snapped my head toward it and immediately knew that something was wrong. I didn't need to see the ruined mascara on Summer's face or hear her sniffling or pay attention to her slouched, victim-like body language.

There was something about having such an unbreakable bond with Summer that helped me understand how she felt at all times even when she didn't utter a single word. Sometimes it was well-concealed, but that night, it couldn't have been clearer.

Through the shuddering, gasping, and weeping, I was able to discern only one, just barely coherent sentence that she uttered into my chest as I held her.

"He raped me."

At first, my brain refused to register the word. I must have misheard it, right? Surely she meant to say something other than that horrific word. But then she repeated the same sentence over and over in a trance as if she knew that I needed to hear it multiple times in order to understand.

Boris Bacic

My hands and feet went cold at that. My little sister, my innocent Summer had been desecrated like that by a scumbag, low-life like Robert? That couldn't possibly be.

These things don't happen to us. We hear about them on the news, but we never expect them to happen to us. There is something about being a victim of such an unspeakable act that kind of kills something inside you.

I honestly would have preferred Robert have raped *me* rather than Summer because it would have been easier for me to deal with the pain and guilt that overwhelmed me. I cried along with her because there was nothing else I could do.

When we were done, we called the police, and then they went on to arrest and charge him. Before we knew it, we were all in court, hoping Robert would be convicted of sexual assault. I couldn't stand seeing his smug face. He practically looked complacent with what he had done. When our eyes met, the corner of his lip contorted into a smile. I could almost hear him saying, "Go on, do what you must. You can't un-rape your sister."

Prison would be a tiny fragment of justice, I told Summer just as I told myself. That was, at least, the thread of hope I held on to. But that justice never came. The defendant was found not guilty due to a lack of evidence. To say that I was livid was an understatement. I was forcibly taken out of the courtroom by the security officers and later fined for contempt of court, which cost me a hefty $600.

Robert had raped my sister and caused her immense mental trauma that way. Summer's boyfriend Matias left after learning about the incident (not a nice guy after all), and that further exacerbated her depression.

All of that, and Robert walked away, a free man.

Gotta love the American justice system.

Summer had already been prepared to give herself closure on this chapter. We all were. Robert serving time in prison would have at least brought Summer an ounce of solace, but that never came.

It was safe to say that Summer had started disintegrating after that. She had become an empty shell of the person she formerly was. I knew that she just needed time to heal, and I saw those moments of healing seeping through the cracks of the surface from time to time, but they were so minuscule that they weren't even worth noting.

It was painful for me to watch her like that. I blamed myself for what happened. I wondered whether I should have been more aggressive in my approach just like Mom and Dad. I wondered if I should have taken the initiative to tell Robert to fuck off and threaten him with a restraining order. I wondered if I should have slapped Summer over and over until she came to her senses.

Too late for regrets and apologies.

Summer would need a long time to recover from the trauma to ever go out on a date again, let alone sleep with another man. All thanks to one person. It seemed like I spent more and more time consoling Summer while she cried in bed than I did focusing on myself. With the stress piling up, both at work and at home, I was reaching my breaking point.

Then, one day, I just up and decided to visit Robert.

2

FIRST BLOOD

I had no idea what I was thinking at the time. This was about five months after the court hearing. I knew where he lived, and I doubted he had sobered up and turned his life around enough to move out of his mother's den, so I just sat in the Dodge, turned the key (it took a few turns to get the engine to start) and drove on a whim. I'd told Summer I had some business to take care of and I'd be back by nightfall.

Robert lived in Medford, near Crater Lake Avenue, which was already a red flag. No, literally, that area is marked as red for violent crimes on the map, which makes it one of the more dangerous areas to live in.

I remember thinking how the name Little Red Riding Hood really fit Summer because she was able to look past all the red flags and not become suspicious. Robert and his mom lived in a shitty rectangular excuse of a house that looked just about ready to crumble if you tossed a pebble at it.

I don't remember what went through my head when I rang the doorbell. It was probably one of those moments where your brain is so focused on what was about to happen that you don't feel anything. Like when you're supposed to have a presentation in front of the entire class, and you feel nervous as hell, but then in the final minute or so before it starts, your mind just goes blank, and you're on autopilot.

That's what it was like for me until I heard the lock of the front door opening.

I expected to see a short, elderly lady opening the door for me. She would have a polite smile on her face and ask

Feel Free To Scream

me how she could help me. She would happily invite me in when I tell her that I came to visit Robert, and she would proceed to tell me how Robert doesn't have many friends and how exuberant she is to have such a nice-looking young woman like me visiting her son.

It was usually like that, wasn't it? The mothers of people like Robert were always polite pushovers. I could almost imagine Robert screaming from the basement, "Ma! Get me another beer!" over the loud rock music, and his mother would listen. Robert would ungratefully grab the beer and remind her to shut the door on her way out.

But the old lady from my vivid imagination never opened the door. Instead, it was Robert himself who greeted me.

His expression of shock was what I imagined reflected on my own face. The slight panic that had formed on his features morphed into a complacent half-rictus as if he was trying hard not to laugh at a joke I was not a part of.

"What do you want?" he asked.

What do you want? The audacity to ask such a thing pissed me off. He had strung my sister on for a whole year and then raped her, and now he had the nerve to ask what I wanted. I pressed my lips tightly to avoid spitting on him. I knew that if I did that, the door would shut in my face, and I would lose my chance to do what I wanted to do. Or maybe worse. Maybe he would rape me, too.

Standing in the rundown neighborhood on that cloudy day, alone, with no one to call for help in the vicinity, I realized just how vulnerable I was and what a foolish decision it was to come here.

"Well, speak up," Robert repeated, his face now laced with slight impatience.

The problem was I didn't know what I wanted. I had driven three hours to visit my little sister's rapist, and I had no idea why I had done it. Come to think of it, I had more than enough time to ponder the whole thing in the car, and yet, my mind was blank then, too.

Time was running out. If this was a video game, I would see countdown numbers hovering in the corner of my vision. Once the countdown reached zero, it would be game over. No checkpoints, no way to reload your progress.

"Can I come in?" was all I was able to mutter with my tied tongue.

Robert stared at me like he was weighing his options. The smirk on his face showed how powerful he must have felt in that moment. He got away with an unforgivable crime, and now the victim's sister stood in front of his door like a drenched puppy, asking to come inside. I didn't even want to imagine the disgusting stirring that must have occurred in his pants.

And yet, I was forced to visualize it because he bit his lip and grabbed his... thing through the trousers while opening the door wider and stepping aside. I didn't know if the gesture was supposed to be seductive because it worked more as a repellant.

Summer, Summer, Summer... I reprimanded her in my head as I stepped into the dimly illuminated house – another thing I did on autopilot. By the time I realized how dangerous such a thing was, the door was already closed behind me, effectively shutting out the sounds of the breeze that I hadn't even realized gave me a feeling of safety.

Robert walked past me and led me deeper into the house. I had to hold my breath as the stench of stale sweat and booze left a trail behind him. He slumped onto the couch in the living room and gave his tool another good rub before ogling me like I was here to fulfill his animalistic desires. I remained entrenched in the middle of the room, refusing to come any closer to him.

I remember wondering if that's how he behaved and felt the night when he raped Summer. Is that what he was

Feel Free To Scream

hoping for now, too? The fear that I had felt slowly simmering in the pit of my stomach was replaced by defiance the moment I looked at his face.

His vainglorious expression woke something up inside me. Summer's innocent, tear-stricken face came into my mind's eye, and that caused white-hot rage to manifest from somewhere—like a volcano that had suddenly erupted.

I was still in control of my emotions, though. Robert probably wanted to see me hurt and angry. He probably got off on it. I was determined not to give him that satisfaction.

"I got some time before Mom comes back from grocery shopping. So what do you want?" he asked.

"Summer's a wreck," I blurted.

It was one of those sentences that you utter just to break the ice and start the conversation, even if it's a meaningless sentence. Robert stared at me for a moment and then shrugged.

"She's not my problem anymore," he said.

I half-expected that kind of reaction, but it still angered me to see him so dismissive. Scum like him were the reason why bad things in the world happened in the first place—because people like Robert were too selfish to consider other people's lives and too cowardly to take accountability for their own actions.

"She was doing really well," I said. "Her studies were going great. She was working a part-time job. She had a boyfriend. Now she can barely get out of bed some days."

Robert shrugged once more. The corner of his lips twitched ever so gently. He was having difficulty hiding that disgusting smile. That's when it hit me just how horrible of a human being he was.

It was one thing to be selfish, but it was completely different to actually enjoy other people's misfortunes. He was happy that he managed to ruin Summer's life. The not-so-subtle grab of his crotch only confirmed that. He wasn't only a piece of shit. He was also a psychopath.

How did Summer, a student of psychology, manage to date a guy like him for over a year and not read him enough to tell that he was incapable of feeling empathy?

Little Red Riding Hood, Mark's voice jeeringly entered my mind.

"Why did you do it?" I asked. "She had a good life. All you had to do was leave her alone. But you went out of your way to call her and meet up with her and to... and for what? Just because she broke up with you?" My voice slightly cracked, but I tried to hide it by gulping. "Because your ego was too hurt?"

"Innocent until proven guilty." Robert threw his hands up, and this time, he hadn't bothered hiding his shit-eating grin.

He stood up, sniffled, and then wiped his nose on the sleeve of his T-shirt. "Why did you come here, huh?"

I didn't like him approaching me, but I refused to backstep. I wasn't going to show this pathetic excuse of a human being that I was afraid of him, no matter how much bigger and stronger than me he was.

Truth be told, I was terrified. Seeing him towering above me and staring at me with that confident grin, and knowing that I was alone with him in the house with no one close to call for in case I needed help, terrified me.

"To be honest, I don't really know," I said, but my voice sounded meek and barely above a whisper.

"You don't know," he jeered. "Well, I'll tell you why you came."

He took another step closer to me, and this time, I couldn't resist the urge to take a step back. It was partially the stench but mostly the fact that I felt threatened by him.

"You came here because you heard stories from Summer. Because you know you want this. Don't kid yourself," Robert said.

He licked his lips—another gesture I found repelling rather than seductive. His hand flew toward his crotch, and he no longer bothered to hide touching himself. I hadn't even realized that I'd been backstepping until my back hit the wall and I had nowhere to run.

Robert's face was rigid with a twisted pleasure. He was going to do to me exactly what he did to Summer. Once it was done, he would continue living his life like nothing ever happened. He might boast to his circle of guy friends about this.

Yeah, so you know that dumb chick I used to date? The one who sued me for rape, yeah. Well, guess what? I fucked her sister, too.

The thought made me sick to my stomach. Had I eaten something during the trip, I'm sure I would have puked it out now. Robert put one hand on the wall beside my head, the other one still on his crotch.

"Stay back," I said, my timbre pleading.

It occurred to me that begging was exactly what he wanted me to do. Robert leaned closer to me, the redolence intensifying and invading my nostrils until they burned. I turned my head away as his warm, putrid breath swaddled my neck.

I imagined my skin shriveling like an old fruit under his breath. I felt his hand touching my blouse, fiddling with the buttons on it.

"You know you came for this. Why else did you come?" he asked. "Now you're going to get it. Feel free to scream. The neighbors here don't care."

My hand instinctively flew toward his face. The slap produced a loud smack that was followed by deafening silence. When Robert looked at me again, he was no longer smiling. His cheek was red, and his features that of shock. As if just then realizing what I had done to him, his face contorted into pure anger.

I'd seen Robert annoyed, but never angry. It was terrifying. In that moment, I knew that escaping would be the only viable option.

Before I could turn around, I felt something heavy colliding with my cheek. The next thing I knew, I was on all fours, my cheek burning and my ears ringing. Then, I was forcibly up on my feet again, my scalp burning with a hot intensity as I realized that Robert was yanking a clump of my hair.

I screamed and clawed at his hands, but his fingers were constricted tightly around my hair, only pulling harder the more I fought. My eyes fell on the bulge in his pants. It was more out of anger and inability to stare at that disgusting thing than survival instinct that I did what I did next.

I swung my foot backward and then kicked as hard as I could. My shin connected with his junk so hard that I was sure—I *hoped*—that something broke there.

A yelp came from Robert, and instantly, the grip on my hair allayed as he grabbed at his crotch and squeezed his legs closer together as if he had to pee really badly. This was my opportunity.

I ran past him while he mulled over his precious instrument. I fell headlong before even reaching the door leading to the foyer. My forehead whacked the floor, once again bringing back the ringing in my ears and, this time, adding bonus dizziness to the vision.

"You fucking bitch!" Robert shouted, his grip on my ankle tightening like a vice.

My nails clawed at the carpet, desperately trying to reach the threshold, but it was futile. In one smooth motion, I was dragged back across the floor a foot or so. Vaguely, I became aware that I was crying. Is this what it had been like for

21

Summer? Was she crying and afraid for her safety while at the mercy of this monster?

I had never actually thought about the act itself. Perhaps it was too hellish for me to imagine it. In my mind, it was a traumatic experience; a forbidden word that caused Summer immeasurable pain. But I never pondered what Summer must have felt like *during* the act.

Now, I was getting a sneak peek.

The more I tried to crawl across the floor, the more I got pulled back. Then, I was rolled over on my back with Robert sitting on me. Any small chances I had of running away were now gone because there was no way I would be able to overpower a man his size, especially when he was on top of me.

I thrashed against him, most of my hits hitting him in the forearms, only a few meagerly connecting with his temples and forehead. If anything, it only made him angrier. I saw him swinging his hand back for momentum, and I knew that same hand would strike me across the face, and yet I was powerless to stop it.

It was like one of those deer-in-the-headlights moments. I was the deer, and Robert was the car. The slap was so hard that all the noises surrounding me became muffled like underwater acoustics.

I didn't know where I was. The next thing I knew, a tearing sound filled my ears, and I felt cold air on my exposed chest. The bastard had ripped open my blouse. That kickstarted me into action again. I pushed against him, but he barely even seemed to notice it.

"I hope you're as vocal as Summer was. I love vocal girls," Robert said as he let out a sadistic cackle.

I swung my entire body to the side as much as Robert's weight on my body allowed me to. He slightly tottered, but not enough to lose balance. One of his bony hands squeezed around my throat while he used the other to undo the belt of my jeans.

"Don't fight, and it'll all be over soon," he said.

I squirmed under his touch. I'd much rather have leeches and snakes down my pants than this man. In a desperate attempt to fight against him, I blindly touched the floor, hoping to find something, anything that could—

My fist closed around a small, tubular object on the floor. I don't know where it came from and how it had gotten there, but in that moment, it was god sent. I worked a corporate job as director of recruiting, which meant I needed to sign a lot of papers every day, which meant I instantly recognized the object in my hand as a pen.

I didn't think about my next move.

I let out a feeble scream, which was about as much as the hand squeezed around my larynx allowed me to do, and swung the pen toward Robert's head. It delectably embedded itself into the side of his neck nearly half of its length. Never in my life have I experienced something so satisfactory.

Back when I was a kid, I loved poking holes into objects with pencils and needles. I used to do it all the time in classes to my eraser, or any wrappers that I happened to be bored enough to straighten, or even certain fruits.

Summer absolutely hated coming into the kitchen and seeing a knife sticking out of the watermelon, but it's just so damn fun to thrust it into the green exterior. Those feelings of fleeting satisfaction were nothing compared to what it felt like when stabbing the pen into Robert's neck.

But that feeling, too, faded in comparison to what happened next.

At first, Robert didn't quite understand what was going on. He could tell something was wrong; that much was clear from his facial expression and the fact that his grip on me loosened, but he didn't know what.

Feel Free To Scream

His hand reached toward his neck and brushed the pen that stuck out, his eyebrows intermittently raising and lowering as if to say "Huh, what's this doing here?". That gave me the surge of confidence I needed, but it also got my anger boiling further.

I grabbed the pen and yanked it out of his neck, causing a spurt of blood to come out in a gush. Robert coughed, the look of power completely gone from his face, and it made me feel so good. I'm ashamed to say that it even turned me on a little to see him display such a pathetic facial expression.

I jabbed the bloody pen at his neck again. He never saw it coming. It went through his skin like a knife through butter. It was satisfying, but not enough. I needed something sharper, something longer. And I needed to stab him in places where he would feel a lot of pain.

Before I knew it, he toppled sideways while gurgling and gasping. I was up on my feet, a concoction of anger, excitement, and righteous indignation swirling inside me. I should have done something, I realized. Either call an ambulance or get out of there, or maybe something completely different.

But I couldn't. I was mesmerized by the sight in front of me. Robert's eyes met mine as he desperately pressed his palms against the holes in his neck, trying to plug them and stop the blood from flowing out. If he could speak, I imagined him pleading with me.

Even if I wanted to help him, which I didn't, it was too late. An abundance of blood had already pooled around his head. He was bleeding out fast, and I hoped he would stay alive just a little longer, to suffer; to see me reveling in his torment.

I heard a laugh of relief which I realized a moment later came from my mouth. It wasn't just relief, either. It was satisfaction. Robert's legs kicked violently, his eyes intermittently darting from me to something on the coffee table. I realized a moment later that it was his phone.

I looked at it then back at him. He didn't seriously expect me to call an ambulance for him, did he? I mean, it would have been the right thing to do, but I had no intention of spending taxpayers' money to waste the EMTs' time so they could save the life of this worm.

"Don't fight and it'll all be over soon," I quoted him, the smile on my face still there as if someone was pulling the corners of my lips with fishhooks.

The tingling between my legs beckoned my hand, but I resisted the insatiable – and unnatural – urge. At that moment, I wanted to savor every moment of Robert's suffering. I wanted to memorize every second of it because the pleasure it gave me was stronger than any orgasm I'd ever experienced in my life. My heart pounded in my chest, and I knew it wasn't just from the physical exertion.

In his final moments, Robert's eyes were fixed on me. The gurgling and the coughing had stopped, the gushing of the blood had stopped, and all fell silent. He was staring right at me. I was the last thing he saw before he died.

I bit my lip to suppress a hysterical peal of laughter. Robert was no longer the powerful man he thought he was. He was just a useless corpse now that could never hurt another human being.

With the intense feeling of pleasure, curiosity also arose. It made me feel a bit like the time I had found a dead pigeon in my backyard when I was five years old. I had poked the dead animal with twigs, probingly at first, but then I punctured it with sharp sticks. It was infantile curiosity, nothing more.

I'm not a monster, and I could never hurt any animals. In fact, before killing Robert, I had considered myself similar to Summer—that I wouldn't hurt a soul. But it's crazy how twisted love for our family members can be sometimes. Robert was a piece of shit that didn't deserve to live, and I had no regrets about doing what I did to him.

Besides, it was self-defense.

That term woke me up like a snap of a finger next to my head. I had just killed a person, and I was most likely going to be charged with first-degree murder. I couldn't think straight. The sexual pleasure I'd felt until then was all but gone, replaced by fear of consequences.

Before I could do anything, I ran to the front door and yanked it open with my blouse (Somehow, my boggled mind managed to remember not to grab the door with my bare hand because of fingerprints).

I ran out of Robert's house, blouse open and droplets of blood on me and all, and hightailed it out of there.

3

ANTICIPATION

I don't remember the drive back to Portland except for the fact that I trembled like a branch in the wind. I desperately needed to get my blouse off, not because it was ruined by Robert and not because it smelled like him, but because it had dried blood on it.

I happened to have a spare sweater on the backseat among the empty bottles of water (thank God for being a slob) which I changed into. I tucked the blouse under the passenger's seat and got rid of it once I was close to Portland by tossing it into a nearby pond.

By then, I was still shaking, but more than anything, realization of what I'd done had finally hit me. Robert was dead. *Dead.* Killed by me. Whenever I blinked, I saw him gurgling on the floor while blood spewed from the tiny holes in his neck. It was supposed to be a satisfying memory, but it only brought me nausea.

Every car I drove by made me paranoid. I thought I could feel the accusatory, penetrating gazes of the other drivers glaring at me. Somehow, my mind had perceived that they knew what I had done, even though that couldn't possibly be true.

My fear grew when I drove past a parked cop car. They were waiting for me. Medford Police had already informed their guys in Portland of a murder and were now waiting to ambush me. One of the cops in the car looked right at me as he spoke something on the radio.

Suspect is a woman in her late twenties, scared shitless, driving a... what is that piece of shit? Is that a Dodge? She's on I-5 and en route to Portland. Over.

10-4. Will apprehend her as soon as she's here.

Those dialogues ran through my head as I expected the blue lights to start flashing behind me along with the blaring siren. I was honestly on the fence about whether I should just pull over, get out of the car, and confess my crime, or hit the pedal to the metal and lead them on a chase.

The latter wouldn't last long, I knew right away. I can't even do proper parallel parking, let alone a police chase. If anything, the resisting would only net me extra years in prison on my already nasty-looking upcoming sentence for murder.

The flashing lights and the siren never came. I know because I stared intently at the rearview mirror—so much that I almost crashed into the Mercedes in front. I didn't breathe a sigh of relief until I rounded the corner and the cops were out of sight. I kept wiping my palms on my jeans, but the clamminess just kept penetrating through my skin.

When I finally parked in front of the apartment and killed the engine, it hit me that I had actually made it home. It was night already, and I knew that Summer must have been worried.

The first thing I did was look up and down the street for any suspicious vehicles—perhaps police cruisers or something that undercover cops might use. But what kind of cars would undercover cops use? Personally, I didn't know the first thing about cars, but if I were a cop, I'd most likely use something that wasn't too garish.

Once I made sure that there were no FBI agents, SWAT units, positioned snipers, or any other armed forces ready to ambush me, I stepped outside the car. The cool air felt good. It helped clear my head, even if it was just a little bit.

I spent a solid five minutes in front of the stairs, heaving in deep breaths, just like I had learned from the Israeli yoga instructor on Instagram. I'd been following her for a while, and her advice seemed good, but the problem was that I only got to try out her tips in calm situations. Now that I was nail-bitingly stressed, I could hear her serene voice whispering specifically to me.

Breathe in. Breathe out. Not so fast. Breathe in slow— no, control your breathing. Calm down— you're not very good at this. Let's take it from the top.

I needed another moment to compose myself in front of the apartment. The doormat with the Harry Potter spell *Alohomora* stared at me from the floor. Once I felt that I was sufficiently presentable for my little sister, I stepped inside the apartment. I half-hoped not to find her there, but of course, whenever you want something to work a certain way, the universe has a way of fucking it up.

Not only was Summer home, but she was right in the living room, so as soon as I opened the door, the first thing that greeted me was her curious stare.

"Hey, where have you been?" she asked. It was obvious that she had been worried about me.

Oh, you know. Just on a drive to kill your ex. The usual.

"Sorry. I remembered that I had something to take care of in the office." The blatant lie that came from my mouth surprised me.

I flashed Summer a meek grin and tossed the car keys on the kitchen counter. My eyes briefly fell on the keys in an *oh shit, what if there's blood on them* moment. There wasn't.

Summer asked me something about ordering takeout and watching a Netflix show, but I felt like doing neither. The mention of food got my stomach rumbling in protest, but the nausea refused to abate, so eating dinner would be impossible tonight. Fine by me. I've been wanting to lose a few pounds anyway, but Summer's incessant hoarding of sweets always foiled my plan.

I excused myself and asked Summer to postpone the plans to another day because I didn't feel too well and wanted to take a long, hot bath. On my way to the bathroom, Summer shot a question that caught me off guard.

"What happened to your face?" she asked.

Crap.

Just as she said it, I felt it—the pain in my cheek from Robert's heavyweight slap. I gently put my hand on the cheek and turned to face Summer, unsure if I should put on a surprised face or tell her right away what had happened.

"Oh, that. I uh... I smacked my face on the door," I said. Another lie that impressed me, no matter how clumsy it was.

Summer didn't seem to suspect anything. Either she was too oblivious (Little Red Riding Hood!) or I was a great actress.

I doubted it was the latter because subtlety wasn't my forte. At least not until then.

I ran the bath and put some of the expensive salts that I'd been keeping for special occasions—like after a business trip or a particularly hard day—into the bathwater. I figured that stabbing someone in the neck with a pen was just as demanding as a business trip or a long day at work and ended up treating myself to a nice bath.

As soon as I was in the water, I felt all my wariness diminishing. It hadn't hit me until then how exhausted I was. Couldn't have been from the fight with Robert, I figured. It must have been the worry and possibly the long drive there and back.

My entire body was sore. I found painful spots on my wrists, my neck, my side, and even the skin on my palms and knees was abraded. The hot water felt good on my injuries, although I assumed it was because I was physically washing myself of Robert's stench and blood.

I closed my eyes and enjoyed the silence. If the cops came storming inside the apartment, then I hoped to at least get fifteen more minutes of this before they cuffed me and dragged me out.

You want to arrest me right now?! I'm in the middle of something; mind waiting outside the bathroom?

I didn't sleep well that night.

For the next few days, I was a wreck. It was as though Summer's and my role had been reversed and now I was the one who needed support. *Even in death, Robert is ruining our lives,* I thought.

I didn't tell Summer what was up, of course. I made an excuse about feeling sick and she believed me. I took a sick leave off work as well. With the contribution I made to the company, they'd better be damn supportive of my days off.

I honestly expected the cops to come knocking on the door any day now. Every time the phone or the doorbell rang, I jumped and thought *this is it.* I had actually prepared myself for it. I knew that it was only a matter of time before they linked Robert's murder with me and that I would be sent to prison for a long time.

At first, the thought was so nauseating that I couldn't digest a bread crumb. But then I sort of started to accept it. *No use mulling over spilled milk,* Dad always said. He mostly used it as an excuse whenever he messed something up with Mom—like when he forgot to take out the trash or broke a glass or a plate, or literally spilled milk—but the point was still relevant.

The cops never came, and what happened instead was that Robert's murder was reported on the news.

I never watch or read the news, especially nowadays since it's all about the Republicans and the Democrats having a dick-measuring contest, but the way I found out about Robert was thanks to Summer.

Feel Free To Scream

It was four days after my visit to Medford, and we had been having breakfast together—sunny-side-up eggs and toast that Summer had made for us because I slept in. While eating, she browsed her phone—she has a habit of burying her nose in her phone pretty much all the time. Whenever we're both at home, I can hear incessant pings coming from the room.

I keep my phone on vibrate only because I don't want to be pestered 24-7, especially by coworkers when I'm not working, and because I'm afraid of becoming addicted to the cell phone like most people nowadays are.

Anyway, we were eating breakfast, and at one point, I told Summer to put down the phone and focus on her food. When I looked up from my runny egg yolk, Summer's eyes were wide as saucers, transfixed on the phone, one side of her cheek bulging from the food in her mouth, but she wasn't chewing.

A part of me knew what caused such a reaction, and yet I still asked her what was wrong. She continued staring at her phone a moment longer, her face vacillating from her healthy skin color to a sickly pallid.

Instead of telling me what was up, she turned the phone so that the screen faced me. The headline *MAN IN MEDFORD FOUND DEAD, POLICE SUSPECT FOUL PLAY* gawked at me. I took the phone from Summer and skimmed through the short article. After reading it once, I read it five more times, my eyes darting across each line as if I somehow thought the text would change while I stared at it.

The gist was that the police had no suspects and they suspected foul play. I'm glad I had a mouth full of eggs because the smile of relief on my face probably would have been obvious. With that feeling of relief also came a need to laugh.

I didn't hold back.

A piece of egg white flew out of my mouth when I chuckled. That turned into laughing until tears formed in my eyes and the muscles in my abs started hurting. Summer stared at me like I was a dangerous, unpredictable lunatic, but I didn't care.

When I was done laughing, I felt like I needed to take a nap even though I had gotten up just recently. Summer was pensively staring down at her plate of half-eaten food. I had finally stopped laughing by then and asked her how she felt.

"I don't know," was all she said.

"You don't know?" I asked.

"I don't know," she repeated. "But I feel... I feel like something heavy just dropped off my heart. I don't want to be happy that someone died, but... I think I am."

"Summer... Robert was a piece of shit. He deserved everything that happened to him. If it were me, I would have tortured him before killing him." I had to press my lips together to suppress another wave of laughter.

"Yeah. I think I'm gonna go for a walk," Summer said.

She looked like a zombie, but she was going to be okay. Maybe Robert's death wouldn't necessarily make her feel better, but it certainly wouldn't make her feel worse. As she left the living room, I mulled over the article, the smile on my face desperately wanting to stretch from ear to ear in the satisfaction with the good deed I had done.

POLICE SUSPECT FOUL PLAY.

Well, yeah. You don't need to be Sherlock Holmes to know that getting stabbed in the neck with a pen isn't exactly suicide.

But they didn't have a suspect. That was really good. That meant that they couldn't find anything on the crime scene they could connect with me. It was pretty much unbelievable. It's the twenty-first century, and criminals can still get away, even with the heavy surveillance and advanced forensics.

Feel Free To Scream

Maybe they just didn't care. Robert was Robert, after all.

The victim is a what? An accused sexual offender? Bag him and let's call it a day.

Then again, maybe they somehow ruled it out as an accident? Either way, just to be on the safe side, I decided to treat the article with a grain of salt and be careful. I didn't want to slip and reveal to Summer or anyone else that I was the murderer. For all I knew, the police might have been following me and I didn't know it.

For now, I would continue living my life as a law-abiding citizen.

4

THE NEWS

The following morning, Summer looked like she had been reborn. The way she strode out of her room, beaming, with a smile on her face and practically skipping to the kitchen, jovially exclaiming "good morning!" to a groggy me, immediately made me see the difference. The only thing missing was some angelic background music with a godly light shining directly on her.

In fact, the whole thing stuck out so much that I lowered the mug of coffee even though it was halfway up to my mouth. Anyone who knows me even a little knows that morning coffee is a sanctity to me; a ritual that absolutely must be followed every morning without fail or interruption.

So, me bringing the mug down even though I was ready to take a sip of the steamy, brown elixir said a lot about my reaction.

Summer and I only exchanged a few words before she told me she was going to walk Mrs. Dott's Labrador and strode out of the apartment with her purse, leaving me dumbstruck in the silence of the apartment. Summer hadn't done that since before the… traumatic event that shall not be named.

Needless to say, seeing Summer happy brought a smile to my face. I felt as though I had just done a really good deed, not just for my sister but for the whole world. It gave me a sense of pride. Getting arrested no longer seemed like the slightest issue. If killing Robert made my sister happy and restored her to her old self, then I would gladly face the consequences of my actions.

I returned to work that same day. I felt like a new woman. I felt like I could tackle the world. I was still prudent about breathing a sigh of relief at the dodged bullet—in this case, the bullet being me getting imprisoned—but I felt really good.

My coworkers greeted me and spewed some fake template questions regarding my health and I answered in an equally fake way. When I first started working as a recruiter, I had to fake-smile so much that the muscles in my cheeks hurt. I had to take active breaks with a resting bitch face to rejuvenate my mouth. Now, I could retain a grin on my face for hours without even noticing it.

In fact, the fake-smiling often bled into my daily life, and that annoyed me. I found myself fake-smiling with strangers, especially in restaurants or at the supermarket. Summer pointed that out, and I tried fixing it, but muscle memory prevailed. Fifty hours of work versus normal human interaction a few times a week—it's clear who the winner was.

I can't say the grimacing was only bad, though. Whenever I had to deal with morons at work, smiling was great to help conceal my anger. Like when a candidate comes to the interview completely underprepared and asks basic questions that they already should have researched before applying to a position in a company like this one; or when a coworker says they didn't receive the email even though I sent it to them (get with the times, Sharon, I CCed you and I don't plan on being your email-forwarding servant because you're too old and lazy to learn the technology); or when someone who'd never have a snowball's chance in hell flirts with me.

How's the project going? Let me know if you need some help with it.

I just received this email from the manager. He says I should send him the spreadsheet now. What do you think I should do?

And the one that ticks me off the most with interviewees: *Can you tell me if I passed the interview?*

For all those frustrating moments, I'd grit my teeth through the fake smile on my face, and it worked really well with other teams, candidates, etc., but those who know me well can tell when I'm about to explode. Ling from HR was vivid in her description of it.

She said that a vein worms on my temple, my gums show too much, my eyes are too wide open, and she mentioned that she saw my cheek twitching a few times. I didn't bother fixing it, even though she gave me a "friendly reminder" to do so for the sake of maintaining a positive working atmosphere.

All of this makes it sound like my job is horrible, and it definitely can be, especially when deadlines are approaching. I had started working here six years ago, and at the time, I had initially planned on leaving to greener pastures someday.

Then the opening for the position of Team Lead came up, and I decided to apply, albeit aloofly. I didn't really want the position, to be honest. There's nothing worse than being in charge of a group of overworked, underpaid people and getting blamed for every tiny mistake they make.

Even the pay wasn't that much higher than the position I had at the time (Senior Sales Representative, which is a fancy way of calling a salesperson whose job was to pester people who didn't have money with offers they couldn't afford). Still, I applied on a whim because it couldn't hurt to try, right?

Superiors gave all the candidates for the position of Team lead a heavy book to study. Seriously, it was so heavy that I felt like whacking someone with it in the head would give them a concussion. I had started skimming through it two nights before the test, but I found that there was too much

Feel Free To Scream

information there written in letters too tiny for me to remember.

I ended up going out to the test unprepared just like the interviewees that I deride so much nowadays. Surprisingly, I knew a lot of answers to the questions on the paper. I was done in a matter of minutes while my rivals (even though I didn't consider them rivals; they could have the job for all I cared) furiously scribbled with focused facial expressions.

Gary, who had also worked as a Sales Representative on my team at the time and had visibly taken a disliking to me because he felt threatened, was sweating profusely. I swear, on my way out, I saw a droplet of sweat falling from the bang of his hair and onto the paper, smudging the ink.

The moment I left the classroom was the moment I forgot all about the test and continued focusing on my daily work. I hadn't even bothered to find out when the test results would be out. The only reason I knew about it was because Noelle from my team hurriedly approached my table during lunch and congratulated me.

At first, I didn't know why she was congratulating me. I still remember that I was eating a particularly good sandwich from Subway, and that's honestly all I wanted to focus on. But then Noelle explained that I had entered the final round of interviews for the Team Lead position. That explained Gary's downcast stare and his unwillingness to communicate properly with me that day.

I went to the final interview only because I still retained the logic of "it can't hurt to try." I figured that I'd get eliminated during this step, especially with so many other ambitious people applying who had made it to the final round—people I couldn't possibly compete with; zealous people who were willing to work hours of unpaid overtime and sacrifice their private lives for the sake of the company.

The final interview came and went, and I gave it no second thought. Just like with the test, I forgot all about it and continued with my work. A few days later, my manager called me into the office. I thought it was about something I had messed up until he brought his hand forward for a handshake.

Everyone on my team pretended to be happy for me, even though I could see the envious glowers in their eyes. Here I was, a person who had applied to the position on a whim and got it while these hardworking fanatics were left working as salespeople with a chance to apply to a higher position in six months.

From there, climbing the ranks became easier. I went from Team Lead to Team Manager to Regional Manager to Director of Recruiting. I honestly started thinking I was simply surrounded by incompetent morons. Either that, or I really managed to charm the interviewers.

Whenever someone asked me to tell them my success story (and I've been asked a lot, especially by new recruits who just joined the company with ambitions to reach my position or go higher someday), I shrugged and told them I just used logic.

And that was the truth. I believe in the phrase "work smart, not hard." While other people in my department are putting in hours and hours of overtime to get a good performance review, I complete everything I need to within my working hours, and once I'm out the door, work is no longer my problem until the next morning at 9 a.m.

The higher-ups expected me to apply to even higher positions someday, but I told them right off the bat that it's wasn't going to happen. The six-figure pay I got from this position, including the amazing benefits coupled with the relatively okay work-life balance were not things I would have liked to relinquish.

In fact, I wanted to focus on my private life a little bit. Now that Summer was doing better, I thought about dating again soon.

Feel Free To Scream

After I returned to work from my sick leave, everything went fine for about a month or so. I had almost completely forgotten about Robert save for the quiet moments at night in my bed when I felt especially aroused (That was a kink I hadn't even known I had.) The media reported nothing on the murder, and police never came to arrest and interrogate me.

Then one Wednesday during lunch break, I saw a commotion in the cafeteria. Boxes of tangerines sat untouched on one of the tables (Wednesdays were always fruit days at the company) while the employees converged at the windows, seemingly mesmerized by something. It honestly made them look like a bunch of teenage boys peeping for the first time on a couple having sex.

I thought there must have been a car crash or something, but I didn't really care enough to look. I sat at one of the many unoccupied tables and opened the plastic container with the tuna salad (I'd been trying to eat healthier.)

Dario, who used to work on the same team as me and was now an IT specialist, asked if he could sit next to me. He didn't seem bothered by the commotion at the windows.

Dario was cool, albeit sometimes annoying and repetitive. He used to be a good spear-thrower, which secured his scholarship and whatnot, and then a knee injury destroyed his dreams of becoming an Olympic athlete.

I found it kind of sad. Looking at Dario was like looking at most of the former-athlete adults who worked in the corporate world. They had these dreams of getting into colleges and building their entire careers, thanks to their athletic abilities, but then either their girlfriends got pregnant prematurely, or they needed the money to support their parents or themselves, or an injury stopped them.

The intense daily workouts that would have them pissing blood would be reduced to mild recreational training, just enough to break a sweat. Five times a week would become three times a week, and then one workout would be skipped because either the day at work was stressful and long or because parental duties called. Until the training was completely eliminated and all that remained were exaggerated stories of glory long since passed.

"What's going on there?" I asked him after the usual small talk.

"Oh, that," he said. "Animal rights activists. They're protesting."

"In front of the company? Why?" I asked as I stuck a piece of lettuce, tuna, and an olive into my mouth.

The texture of the lettuce on my tongue made me feel sorry for the animal rights activists who I assumed were vegans or vegetarians. Luckily, the tuna was here to compensate for the lack of quality protein.

"There was a guy who tortured and killed dogs and cats. Did some really nasty things, too. Like, stuck firecrackers in cats' asses and strung dogs up on trees," Dario said with no more concern than he would "good morning."

"What?" I asked as soon as the bite was chewed enough for me to swallow it. The salty taste of tuna lingered on my lips. "That's terrible!"

I couldn't, for the life of me, imagine what kind of a monster could ever think about hurting such affectionate beings.

"Yeah. Anyway, the guy got off with a fine, and naturally, people are now pissed," Dario said.

I hadn't really given it a second thought until I was done with work. When I exited the building, the booming of the indignant crowd greeted me. There weren't many of them: maybe fifty altogether, but it was enough to block the road.

I never participated in any protests, and I try to steer clear of them (or any loud, chanting crowds) as far as I can when I hear them on the street, so being caught in the throng like this was something new for me.

Just as I thought, most of these people were young, but I could see a few elderly folk among the crowd, vigorously lowering and raising their "STOP ANIMAL CRUELTY" and "JUSTICE FOR OUR FURRY BABIES" signs. Some of them blew into whistles, piercing the air with the blaring sound that threatened to cause me a migraine.

The rows of cars that had been trying to get home from a long day of work were blocked by the crowd, and no matter how long they sat on their horns, the animal rights activists refused to move.

For a moment, all I did was observe the crowd in fascination, wondering what went through the minds of those activists. I could understand the young ones who had come to the gathering.

They were still young and needed to feel like they were a part of something bigger. These gatherings gave them a purpose even if they didn't necessarily believe in it. But what about the old geezers?

Maybe they were here because their pet was one of the victims. Or maybe they had no families and nothing better to do and were looking for acceptance in a crowd of like-minded strangers.

I never believed in protests. I've read about them happening all over the world—in some countries peacefully, in others causing fully armored riot police units to come down on the rebels—but I don't think I've ever heard of a protest changing something. At least not something big. I've always been of the belief that, if a government doesn't want to budge about something, it won't.

I jostled between the people, trying to reach my parked car. A woman in her thirties stepped in front of me with a notepad and a pen shoved into my face. I couldn't discern what she was saying, but based on the gestures, she wanted me to sign something. I politely shook my head, flashed her the PR grin that I'm so used to making, and made my way out of there.

I would later learn that the protests became violent toward the end and a fight ensued between one of the angry drivers who was on his way back to his kid's birthday. The animal activists were upon him as soon as he landed the first punch on the guy in his face. This caused the police to get involved and arrest multiple people.

I had completely forgotten about the whole thing and went on with my life until I got back home from work about a month later to see Summer crying. My first thought was *oh no, someone did it to her again.*

It took her a while to be able to speak up, but once she finally did, it was just like that night when Robert raped her. She uttered only one sentence, barely perceptible at first, and then repeated it over and over, drilling it deeper into my brain.

"Someone poisoned Bella," she said.

Bella was our parents' Pitbull, but Summer and I considered her ours as well, even though we went out to visit our parents only once every few months. The news came as such a shock to me that I thought, for a moment, Summer must have been screwing with me. I refused to believe that Bella, the dog that all the children in the neighborhood knew and loved, was dead.

I called my parents to confirm the situation. The four of us—even Dad, who I'd never seen crying—wept together until we could weep no more.

Feel Free To Scream

5

RESOLVE

I hadn't realized how attached we had all become to Bella until she was no longer with us. Our family had had a Dachshund named Charlie that had joined us when I was two years old and died when I was seventeen—had to be put down due to multiple health issues.

Even after spending my entire childhood and adolescence with Charlie, losing him didn't feel like such a big deal. I was sad, yes, but nowhere near as sad as when we had lost Bella. I could see that the effect was transferred onto my family, too.

Perhaps it was the difference in Charlie and Bella's nature and behavior that made us grow attached to the Pitbull more.

Charlie was a natural hitman. There was no way anything could get inside the backyard without him noticing it. A lot of the mornings on my way to school, I would see a dead bird, cat, mouse, and even toad nestled on top of the neatly trimmed lawn. Animals weren't Charlie's only victims. Pretty much everyone who had come to visit the family was bitten at least once by Charlie. Hell, even Summer and I got bitten once – gently, but still.

It was like a rite of passage.

Bella, on the other hand, despite her looks, was very smart, very gentle, and very affectionate. She learned tricks pretty fast, even ones that we never intended to teach her. There were times during winter that we would let her inside the house, and after spending time with her, we coaxed her into going back outside by offering her a treat.

She was clever enough to memorize the word "treat" and what it means, and as soon as she heard it, she'd be at the door, waiting for us to open it and give her the reward. We had to be careful about uttering that word in her presence.

She had also never hurt another being in her life. Even when we played, simply yelping or saying "ow" was enough for Bella to go from gently biting to licking. Kids all loved her, too. No matter how rough they were with her, she never once complained or did anything to hurt them. In fact, my dad often said that she was more of a cat than she was a dog.

She was only five years old when she died, and the vivid description my mom conveyed through tears haunts me to this day.

She talked about how she heard Bella squealing and whimpering. When they got outside, she walked funny and then vomited blood. Within minutes, she was having a seizure on the grass, and my dad rushed her to the vet. They were too late to save her.

For two days, pretty much everything I'd seen reminded me of Bella. That's how things usually work. You don't notice these things in your daily life until you lose a loved one, and then suddenly, everything reminds you of them.

It occurred to me that I should take a few more days off from work, but I felt like sitting at home doing nothing would only cause my sadness to swell. The fact that I kept looking up "pet died from poison" didn't help me at all.

I don't know why I did it, but it wasn't morbid curiosity. I felt like I needed some closure but also consolation. I wanted to know that Bella wasn't in too much pain. I wanted to hope that the poison simply knocked her out and then put her into a peaceful everlasting sleep.

It didn't.

Most of the poisons caused excruciating deaths, and Bella's was no exception. That only made me feel worse. I felt like my eyes had completely dried out and could produce no more tears. It took everything in me to keep my composure at work.

My coworker Cindy, who had noticed something was wrong with me, coaxed me into telling her what was up. When I told her it was the family dog that had died, she exhaled with visible relief and said "Oh, you should get a new dog." The image of me stapling her mouth shut went through my mind in that moment.

Oh, sure, Cindy. Why don't I get a new dog? It's just a dog after all, right? Why don't you just make another baby after your first one was miscarried?

I knew it wasn't fair to compare babies to dogs, but I couldn't help my anger. Instead of shutting her mouth with the stapler, I opted to turn around and leave.

On the third day after Bella's death, something clicked in my mind. I went from feeling sad to feeling resolved, even though I didn't know about what, exactly.

I called my parents to find out precisely what had happened.

The fact was I already had an idea of who the culprit was, but I wanted confirmation on the subject. Across from my parents' house lived a grumpy old neighbor named Seymore MacGuffin. If that's not a villain's name, I don't know what is.

Seymore hated just about anything and everything, but he seemed to have a special hate for animals—called them useless walking factories of shit, and the few times that Bella approached him amicably, he shooed her away.

Although our family didn't interact with him a lot, it was inevitable sometimes because the houses were just across from each other. The old man hadn't changed a bit for the entirety of my life that I'd known him. He already looked like he was eighty years old when I was a kid. Now I was an adult, and he still looked the same age.

The reason why I thought Seymore was the one who poisoned Bella was because multiple pets from the neighborhood had already died because of him throwing poison around.

I warned my parents multiple times to check the area before taking Bella for a walk, and to call the cops on the old man, but they didn't think it would help.

MacGuffin exclaimed multiple times how he would have poisoned and skinned all the dogs if it were up to him. I also remembered him saying that he has a ton of rodenticide in his basement and that he would not be afraid to use it if any dog came near his property. I was sure it was the same poison he'd thrown around the area just because he could.

My mom confirmed that, yes, Bella had run toward the old man's property and that she had taken something into her mouth before returning. But all of that happened in less than a minute; that was the most terrifying thing of all.

My dad went on to confront Seymore about it, and he confirmed that he had poison around his backyard but that it was used for rats and raccoons. My dad threatened to sue the old man but was sure it wouldn't really do much—it certainly wouldn't bring Bella back.

No, the justice system would do no justice here. Bella was a part of our family and Seymore MacGuffin had killed her. He was a murderer, and there was no way around it.

I found myself fantasizing about doing terrible things to the old man. I had to bite my lip to curb the exuberance it made soar within me. I had remembered Robert, who seemed like such a distant memory now, but the scene of him writhing on the floor in those final moments was forever etched in my mind's eye.

I'd be lying if I said I wanted to kill MacGuffin only because he deserved it. There was also pleasure in that act, but that was only a bonus. A huge bonus at that. I continued looking up online pets' death by poisoning because I was determined to hold onto my anger.

One thing I learned about myself during those days was that I could suppress all the negative emotions that made me feel weak (like sadness and depression) and replace them with anger and the conviction for justice, which made me feel powerful.

I went from only fantasizing about killing the old man to wondering what it would take to pull it off without getting caught, to actually planning it in my mind. The transition was so gradual that by the time I reached the final stage, it was like a train at full speed that I could no longer stop.

I was resolved to end the old man's life before he caused more damage. I kept telling myself that this was the right thing to do, that I was doing something good for the world. After the old man was dead, no more families would suffer losses of their pets because of him.

One Friday, I suggested to Summer that we go visit our parents in Tacoma, Washington. By then, the pain of Bella's passing had faded somewhat, but I knew it would return full force as soon as we were there.

I was ready. Paying respects to Bella wasn't the main reason for suggesting the visit to my parents' place.

This time, I actually went prepared. I went out and bought a box of latex gloves (black, of course, because it was only appropriate for the occasion), pepper spray, and a taser. I bought all three in separate stores because I didn't want the cashiers to give me weird looks.

I went through all the possible scenarios in my head. I knew that there was no way the plan could be one hundred percent fail proof, but honestly, I don't think I cared then.

I remember asking myself at one moment if I was really going to go through with this. The feeling of immense disappointment at the thought of not actually doing it was answer enough for me.

Feel Free To Scream

Summer and I drove out to Tacoma Friday night with the intention of staying there until Sunday afternoon. I tried to remain chatty during the ride to our parents' place, mostly to keep the suspicion off me. I then figured that Summer probably wouldn't have figured what I was up to even if I wore a balaclava and held a garrote wire in my lap.

We had a heartfelt greeting with my parents, even though I had done it absent-mindedly. My gaze gravitated toward the old man's house, maybe even a little too much. The dog killer was nowhere in sight, but I could imagine him sitting somewhere inside the old house, watching his TV blasting on full volume because he was too deaf to hear it otherwise.

Friday went by without a hitch. Saturday as well. I tried to spend a social day with my family, but secretly, I kept an eye on the old man's house. I had seen MacGuffin come out of the house once or twice, always suspiciously squinting up and down the street as if he expected to see someone there, running off with his mailbox torn from the ground.

In order to execute my plan, I needed some privacy. So, I suggested that the whole family go bowling together Saturday night. I had already reserved a spot for us, but when the time came, I told my family I wasn't feeling too well.

My mom insisted they stay home, but I gave her the old "oh, don't let me ruin your fun" excuse, and they agreed to go without me. I watched in excitement as the car pulled from the driveway and drove off, its roaring engine fading in the distance.

It brought butterflies to my stomach just like when I was a teen with wild hormones and just waiting for the house to be empty so I could browse my dad's old porn magazines in secrecy.

Back then, I didn't really understand the fullness of the graphic images on those pages, but they brought a tingling sensation between my legs, which brought me both confusion and pleasure. It wasn't long after then that I found out I could use my fingers down there to intensify the feeling.

As soon as the house and the street were quiet, I began my preparations. I knew I had at least one whole hour before they'd return, but I wanted to use every minute as well as I could.

I've always been a self-starter, and when it came to deadlines, I prefer finishing something as soon as possible and then chilling for the rest of the day than doing last-minute work the night before.

The gloves and taser were already in my purse, ready to be used. I didn't have an actual murder weapon, but that would come later. I pressed the button on the taser to see if it would work. It crackled loudly and produced a bright blue light too close to my face. I slightly jumped back.

I decided needed to be careful with it because the last thing I wanted was to tase myself and lose the opportunity to exact Bella's revenge. I went outside and walked across the road toward the old man's house.

The street was empty, the chirping of the crickets resounding all around me. My heart pounded as I stepped on MacGuffin's precious territory and sauntered toward his house. I remembered how he yelled at me a few times when I was a kid and I ran home crying to my parents. I also remembered how he used a needle to puncture my favorite balloon because it bothered him how it swayed above me.

The lights were on in his house, which must have meant he was home.

Of course he was—where would the old bat go?

I found myself questioning once again whether this was the right thing to do, but just like when I met with Robert, it was like I was on autopilot. I could no more control my feet going toward the house than I could control my heartbeat.

Feel Free To Scream

Before I knew it, my finger was pressing the doorbell, creating a muffled *ding-dong* inside the house. Silence proceeded, deafening and full of suspense. I wondered if the old man was already asleep.

Old people go to bed at the most ridiculous times and wake up before the chickens do in order to use their leaf blowers or lawn mowers and wake up the whole neighborhood. MacGuffin was no exception in that, by the way.

The door opened, and the shriveled old man stood facing me.

The drumming in my chest had all but stopped. The butterflies in my stomach were still here, now somewhat stronger, just like I felt before a blind date or an important event where I needed to perform in front of an audience.

My mouth stretched into a grin.

6

CURIOSITY

Seymore MacGuffin frowned and squinted at me, his lips tucked between his teeth with a grimace that only further brought out the flaws on his face. The few strands of hair that he had left on his spotted head were combed sideways to cover his bald top. It was about as useful as spitting on a raging bonfire.

"Do you know what time it is?" the old man asked with a gruff voice.

My eyes fell on the hand he held on the doorframe. His fingers were long and bony, the knuckles on them so hairy that the tufts looked like they could get entangled. His hand trembled violently. I would have felt sorry for the old bastard had I not known what he'd done to Bella and the other animals.

It wasn't just the animals, either. I'd heard stories about MacGuffin throughout my life from my dad and the other neighbors. He was apparently really selfish, to an extent that he didn't leave his children and grandchildren anything even though he was filthy rich. How he became rich was beyond me, but the house he lived in wasn't too ostentatious, so I figured he must have kept a stash somewhere.

In fact, I imagined him sneaking every night to the corner of the room where he would pull out the fake flooring and marvel at the metal box full of cold hard cash, muttering something along the line of "It's all mine, mine, mine."

"You probably don't remember me, Mr. MacGuffin. I'm the daughter of Bill and Regina," I said and flashed him my PR grin. When I noticed the old man staring at me with an expression like he was trying to remember something really

Feel Free To Scream

important, I hooked a thumb at the house behind me and added, "Your neighbors? Bill and Regina from across the street?"

The old man looked at the house with an equally confused stare. He raised a hand a scratched his flabby cheek. I didn't bother hiding that the smile had drooped from my face. I was starting to lose patience with the old fucker.

If things continued at this pace, by the time we sat in the living room, my family would have finished bowling five times. MacGuffin looked away and retreated one step into the house.

"Don't you young people have any respect for your elders?" he said, the face of confusion morphing into the only other face I'd known on him – grumpiness.

"I'm terribly sorry for bothering you at this time. I only wanted to talk. Would you mind if I come in for a few minutes?" I asked.

It was more my persona from work talking instead of me.

"No. And don't bother me again," MacGuffin said as he grabbed the door's edge, ready to close it in my face.

Something just snapped inside me. It's like when your back is carrying too much weight for a long time and it's warning you that it won't be able to take much more. However, you ignore it, and then it just snaps. That's what happened to my anger filter.

I slammed a palm on the door, effectively stopping the old geezer from closing it. He jerked his head toward me, his eyes wide in surprise.

"That wasn't a request, Mr. MacGuffin," a voice said, and then I realized it belonged to me.

The sentence startled even me nearly as much as the old man. I was still on autopilot, though, and I had no intention of turning back.

"Get off my property before I call the poli—"

MacGuffin never managed to finish that sentence because my hand had already reached inside my purse for the taser and zapped the old man with it. His entire body spasmed epileptically, and he toppled sideways, groaning and moaning in pain.

I took that moment to let myself in. I looked left and right down the street to make sure it was empty before closing the door. I would need to wipe the door later to remove the fingerprints. Even as I put on my gloves, the old man continued moaning feebly on the floor.

He was so puny. He was going to be an even easier target than I initially assumed. I guess I had the wrong kind of assumption about the old man as far as physical strength goes. Back when I was a kid, he looked much bigger and stronger, but then again, everything seemed big from that perspective.

I had to remind myself that I was no longer the scared little kid that I was when MacGuffin popped my balloon and yelled at me to go home. No, I was an adult now, and it was time he faced judgment for everything bad he had done.

"I'm calling the police!" MacGuffin said from the ground.

I found it ridiculous that he was so cocky even when he was so powerless on the ground like that. But I also detected fear in those eyes, specifically when his gaze fell on the gloves.

I turned around and made sure to lock the door. I pulled the key out and put it into my pocket. Nowhere to run now. My heart pounded again, but I was running on pure, unadulterated adrenaline.

"What are you doing?" MacGuffin asked.

"You killed my dog, Mr. MacGuffin. I want to know why," I calmly said.

MacGuffin's mouth contorted into various shapes as if he contemplated what the right thing to say would be.

"Why?! Why did you kill my dog?!" I shouted.

Feel Free To Scream

Tears blurred my vision. I hadn't realized how angry I was until I started shouting. So much suppressed pain and anger, just bursting to get out of me. It would, soon enough. I would delay it a little more, and that would make the feeling stronger later on, like orgasming after days of edging.

"Where's your rat poison?" I asked.

"What are you going to do?" the old man asked.

"Where is it?!" I demanded.

He immediately pointed somewhere and muttered meekly, "In the basement."

I rushed in the direction he pointed. His basement was a small room with one shelf stacked with various products. He had a lot of rodenticides—way more than one person would need for a lifetime.

I wondered what kind of a person keeps rodent poison in such quantities—even if they had an enormous rodent problem. One would think MacGuffin was preparing to declare war on the entire species of rats.

I dug my gloved hand into the bag of rodenticide and took out a handful. It looked like tiny pink candies. A kid could have easily spotted it on the street, scooped it up, and put it into their mouth. They'd die quickly.

When I returned to the entrance, MacGuffin was on his feet, fumbling with the door knob. I raised the taser above my head and demonstratively pressed the button, which made it emit electricity. The old man recoiled even though I was ten feet away from him.

"Please..." he said.

If he was trying to get me to let him off the hook by begging me, he was failing because it only further made me want to kill him.

"Show me your living room, Mr. MacGuffin," I said. "Now," I added when I saw him eyeing me up and down.

He waddled toward the living room and stopped in front of the coffee table before turning to face me. His face was riddled with fear, and I loved every moment of it. There was nothing more satisfactory than seeing a cocky villain losing control.

I've always had that ineffable feeling when watching movies and reading books. Whenever there was a villain I really hated, I put myself in the protagonist's shoes, and I wondered what path I'd choose. I always chose the path of violence: no "I forgive you because it makes me as bad as you," no "I don't want to pursue revenge because it won't satisfy me."

No, the movies that especially gave me a warm feeling inside were the ones where the evildoer who had hurt so many people suffered a gruesome death. To be able to actually put myself in the shoes of the protagonist and exact that justice was overwhelming.

"Sit down, Mr. MacGuffin," I said.

The old man did as I asked.

"Please... I have a family," he said.

What family? The one you alienated because you didn't want to share your money with them, you selfish prick? The family that didn't care enough to visit you more than once every few years?

I wasn't going to give him a grandiose speech or anything like that. I watched enough James Bond movies to know that that's when the captured person manages to buy themselves enough time to give the villain a slip.

But I wasn't the villain here. I was Batman, and MacGuffin was a petty criminal. I just realized that I mentioned superheroes a few times already. I don't even like superheroes; I just thought it would be a great reference.

I placed the taser in my purse. Then, I took a fervent step toward MacGuffin, squeezed him by the throat, and

Feel Free To Scream

watched as his mouth opened in a mute scream. That worked perfectly because I used the other hand to shove the rodent poison into his mouth.

The old man coughed and choked, but I firmly held a hand over his mouth while he thrashed against me. I remember feeling grateful that I decided to use a long-sleeved shirt because he wouldn't be able to scratch my skin and possibly get some DNA under his nails.

After ten seconds or so, I let go and took a step back. The old man coughed, spewing tiny bits of saliva-covered poison on the coffee table and the floor. He looked up at me with wide eyes, grabbing at his throat, realization draping his face at the poison he had swallowed.

We stared at each other in silence for a moment, and then he stood up. The moment he stood up, he fell back down onto the couch, coughing tiny trickles of blood. Veins bulged on his neck, and he let out an agonizing scream, interrupted by another coughing fit.

It ended far too quickly. I watched in relish as the old man coughed more and more blood, which ran down his sweater. And then he fell sideways on the couch and ceased all movement, his eyes wide open, staring into empty space just like Robert's.

I so wished that I could take a picture right then and there, but any form of evidence was too risky. I felt unsatisfied. I had such high expectations for the kill, but it fell somewhat short on my scale like interrupted sexual intercourse.

Why didn't the son of a bitch suffer more? Why did he have to die so quickly? There was a feeling of emptiness inside me that I couldn't quite convey in words. The deed was done, and that made me happy, but I felt like the rush wasn't as great as I expected it to be.

Either way, I was running out of time. I took wet wipes out of my purse and wiped the door and the key before sticking it back into the keyhole. I exited the house and closed the door behind me, and when I returned to my parents' place, I burned the gloves and the sweater in the fireplace.

I was shivering the entire time, but it wasn't from the cold. In fact, I couldn't tell if it was a good kind of shiver or not. I needed another hot bath, so I treated myself to it while replaying MacGuffin's final moments in my mind.

I almost forgot to fake feeling sick when Summer and our parents came back home. The following day, we went back home. No one had suspected anything before we left. Hell, no one even looked toward the old house across the street.

Summer asked me on the ride back why I had a smile on my face.

"Just feeling good about how we spent the weekend," I replied curtly.

Little Red Riding Hood went through my head as I glanced at my sister while I suppressed my laughter.

Killing old MacGuffin wouldn't return Bella, but it sure as hell would deliver a sliver of much-needed justice. MacGuffin's dead body hadn't been discovered until about a month later when passersby started complaining about the smell. So much for having a family.

The police ruled the case as a home accident caused by the old man's dementia, and no further questions were asked. I certainly found it believable enough. If there was an online photo of an old man senile enough to eat a bucket of paint, thinking it was yogurt, then I don't see why the same couldn't be done with rat poison as candy.

Case closed, happy ending.

But killing the old man had confirmed to me that I was far from done. Although I hadn't wanted to admit it, MacGuffin was only a prelude, a test to satisfy my curiosity—to find out whether I was really cut out for this stuff or if I just had a twisted kink.

Feel Free To Scream

    Now, I was ready to undertake more ambitious projects. Just like with work, I wasn't happy staying in one spot for too long. I had to progress and move up in the ranks, whatever the ranks were in this line of work.

    MacGuffin was dead, but there was the animal torturer in Portland who was still on the loose, and I had to make sure that justice prevailed. I finally started to understand those animal activist protesters and their passion for saving animal lives, but they were *praying at the wrong church*, as my dad would always say.

    If you want something done, you need to take matters into your own hands.

7

APPLES

Unlike when I killed Robert, killing MacGuffin didn't make me feel sick. It sent butterflies to my stomach but the good kind. I also didn't question myself as I did with Robert. For a few days after my first kill, not only was I worried about whether I would be caught, but I also kept thinking about whether there was something I could have done differently.

Not that I cared whether Robert lived or died—screw him. But I didn't know at the time if I wanted any blood on my hands, no matter who the person in question was. That feeling allayed rather quickly, and once I was sure that the police didn't suspect me of the murder, I could let loose and enjoy the triumphant feeling.

It was right after killing MacGuffin that I knew my life's calling; one that I'd been looking for all this time but had been unable to find. One that had been right under my nose.

When I was a kid, I wanted to be a prosecutor because of my conviction for justice.

I went through most of my adolescence thinking I really wanted to become a prosecutor only to find out, when the time came, that I didn't want it badly enough to have my nose buried in books for several hours a day and spend sleepless nights cramming before tests.

I never was a person who liked studying and learning new things. I was good in school, but that was only because of my ability to memorize stuff from class and not because I studied at home.

I still remember how my peers in UP constantly complained about having to study for five to six hours every

Feel Free To Scream

day while I barely pulled off an hour on a good day. It put a lot of pressure on me to know that I was one of the only ones who didn't spend too much time studying and stressing over exams.

When I passed with flying colors (even better than most of the nerds and professors' pets who constantly went above and beyond during lectures) I realized that I'd been stressing over nothing.

This raised a lot of eyebrows with the other students. None of them believed that I studied as little as I claimed. You know how there's always that one student who says they didn't study at all and then gets an A-plus on the test? Well, that was me most of the time. I wasn't labeled a nerd, though.

I was pretty much on autopilot through most of my college days. Come to think of it, it was similar to the way I decided to kill Robert—all done on instinct or something like that.

By the time I was a sophomore, becoming a prosecutor was only a distant memory. I had grown up and entered the adult world where nothing was the way it seemed when I was younger.

All I heard around me was that I should get a job, have stability, take a loan from the bank, and buy a house at an inflated price; pay mortgage and taxes. There was, of course, the mandatory "Meet a nice guy, and give birth to his babies," but that was mostly from the older generations.

By the time I graduated, I was pretty much just going with the flow. Any remnants of ambitions I used to have were long gone, and I was more or less getting by. Looking back now, I can't help but scold myself for being that way. I was tucked into this cocoon of safety, working my office job and waiting for the time to pass as if I was waiting for something big to happen.

And it did happen, but not in a way that I expected it.

The accidental murder of Robert the Rapist turned my life around and returned the spark for justice that I used to have. That night, when I looked myself in the mirror, I saw that same young girl with the ambitions to become a prosecutor, who wanted to bring justice to the world.

I knew then that the only reason why I wanted that job was because I had felt that I needed to be a part of something bigger—something that would help me enact my justice. But I was wrong.

As I said before—if you want something done the right way, you've gotta take matters into your own hands.

So that's what I did with James Carter, aka the Animal Torturer.

I spent a while investigating him online. I first checked out the news. There were pictures of mutilated animals alongside the picture of the perpetrator and his full name. It wasn't difficult to locate him since all his information was out in the open. Thank God for social media and lack of online privacy. James was a guy one year younger than me. The pictures he had on Facebook and LinkedIn were not very flattering, and he pretty much looked the way I expected an animal hater to look.

No, he didn't have long, greasy hair like Robert. I don't know why, but whenever I think of pedophiles, groomers, drug addicts, or anything like that, the first thing that comes to my mind is a person with long, unkempt hair.

James had a buzz cut, which only brought out the features of his round head. The goatee, which I'm sure he thought was an awesome idea and that he was rocking it, looked like it was plastered to a pig's ass because it was difficult to tell where his chin began.

The pictures he had taken of himself on social media were very boomer-like. You know, one of those where the photo is taken from a close-up, in a dark room, from a relatively lower angle, while retaining a serious facial expression.

One quick inspection of his profile was enough to determine that the contents he posted were full of made-up quotes from fictional characters that he somehow thought related to him—and all of them were bullshit like being a lion in a world full of sheep, etc.

Seeing all of it physically made me cringe.

He worked at PetSmart for a few months before getting fired (surprise, surprise). Gerbils had apparently been disappearing during his shift, and when they reviewed the footage, they saw him grabbing them and taking them out of the camera lens view. Who knows what he did to them off-camera.

He was now employed at Trader Joe's, although it didn't say what position he worked. I assumed either a cashier or something else low-paying. Since I had almost everything I needed, I decided to go to Trader Joe's (I had some grocery shopping to do anyway.) I knew it was a long shot for me to meet him there, but it couldn't hurt to try.

The atmosphere at the store varied wherever you looked. If you looked at the middle-aged lady cashier scanning the items, you'd say she'd been dead inside for a while. If you looked at the young twenty-something-year-old stacking the shelves and humming while jovially offering his help to customers who looked lost, you'd think this was his dream job.

And then there was the fruit section where a lonesome, overweight guy with a buzz cut and a goatee stood in front of the stand with oranges, not-so-eagerly waiting for the shoppers to hand him the grocery bags so he could weigh them on the scale.

James Carter was even less pleasing to the eye in person than on social media, I noticed right away. Between the stained apron that made his stomach stick out in front of him even more than it probably should and the acne-riddled face, Carter looked like all he needed was a trench coat and a fedora to complete the stereotypical online profile of a nice guy who constantly got friend-zoned and then bitched online about how women always chose the assholes.

In fact, when I approached him, I fully expected him to bow his head down and say "m'lady" in a white-knight fashion that would bring bile from my lunch back to my throat.

He didn't seem to notice me until I was quite close to him. The smell of oranges, mixed in with something less pleasant, invaded my nostrils, and I was sure the stench came from the fat guy.

"Hi," I said amicably, doing my best not to wrinkle my nose at the impending interaction.

James jerked his head toward me, his face of bemusement morphing into a wide-eyed stare that I couldn't identify. Could have been terror, could have been shock that a woman actually decided to speak to him, could have been the sheer amazement at the incomprehensibility of my physical beauty.

I like to think it was the last one.

"Uh, hi," James said with a nasally voice that immediately reminded me of Steve Urkel from Family Matters.

I expected him to add something to the "Uh, hi," but nothing ever came. Not even a, "How can I help you," or "What do you need," and that quickly made me realize that I would need to be the one leading this conversation.

"I want to buy some apples, but I don't know how it works. Do I need like a grocery bag or something, and how do I weigh them?" I asked.

I lied, of course. Although handling the scales could be a pain at times when they plaster the wrong code to it, only a moron wouldn't know how to buy fruits at a grocery store.

"Um..." James looked around as if I had just asked him to calculate the root of a huge number and not how to buy fruits. "Yeah, you can grab a grocery bag, put as many things as you want inside, and then bring them here, and I'll weigh them for you," James said with surprising eloquence compared to the first two or three words he had uttered.

Even before finishing the sentence, he averted his gaze and pretended to have his attention caught somewhere to the side where nothing was happening.

He's shy. He's afraid of girls, I thought to myself while suppressing a conniving smile.

"Actually, would you mind doing it for me? I'm really slow with that kind of stuff, and you look like you have... dexterous hands," I said as I brushed his stubby fingers and smiled.

I was sure that if I had a mirror in front of me, I'd see the vein bulging on my forehead at how hard I was trying not to gag at the touch of his leathery skin. James's hand recoiled, and then he smiled shyly.

I'm usually pretty good at flirting, but the smell wafting from James was distracting. Still, my pathetic flirtation remarks were actually working, which was a testament to how rarely James spoke to women, especially pretty ones like me.

He practically stumbled over himself to do this knight-in-shining-armor favor for this customer in need. Woe is me, I can't handle evil apples; thank you so much for saving me, O Knight of the Grocery Store.

He put a bunch of apples inside the bag, weighed them for me, and plastered on the sticker that came out with the weight and price.

"Here you go," he said with a proud smile.
"Thank you so much," I said as I took the bag from him.
"Not a problem. That's what I'm here for," he said as if he had just saved my life by stopping a train in its tracks, instead of simply weighing a bag of apples. "If you need anything else, I'll be here."
"I appreciate it."
"Anything you need, just feel free to say it. In fact, I can help you buy other things if you need it. Just holler and I'll come running right away."
I smiled, but in my mind, I made the facial expression of the popular meme of a cat coughing in disgust. All I did was ask him to give me some apples, and he was already needy as hell. I couldn't imagine what it would be like to be in a relationship with a person like him.
"Actually, there's one more thing..." I said as I took a step closer.
The smell from before intensified. I couldn't pinpoint what it was; only that it was unpleasant. I ran a finger down his nametag and looked up at him.
"James," I whispered his name seductively.
James gulped. Even through the numerous chins, I could see his Adam's apple bobbing up and down. He had probably never made it this close to a woman before, and he didn't know what to do now. I could almost imagine him getting a nosebleed from forming an erection just from this meager interaction.
"An-anything," he said, all red in the face.
"Can I have your number?" I said as I bit my lip.
I couldn't help but be proud of myself for acting in what I thought was such a convincing manner. It certainly convinced James Carter, even if he was most likely oblivious to any subtle signs of disgust that I'd let slip.
"M-my number? You mean like, my phone number?"
No, your shoe number, you fucking idiot.

"Yeah." I nodded. "You went out of your way to help me with my grocery shopping, and I want to repay you somehow."

I had pulled my hand back from his nametag and twirled my hair around my finger. I doubted he knew that it was usually a sign of a girl liking a guy, but it just felt like the right thing to do in accordance with my acting.

"I um... I actually... I have- I have a girlfriend," James said and tucked his lips into his mouth.

He looked like he had a lot of difficulty uttering that. I tried to maintain the same facial expression, even though I wanted to say "wow" in amazement because who in the ever-loving hell would date someone like this?

Animal cruelty aside, the lack of any physical appeal riddled with bad hygiene and nearly no self-esteem made nothing about this man attractive. She must have been either really desperate or saw something in him that she valued a ton. I couldn't, for the life of me, see anything redeeming enough that would make me want to stay near him, let alone... no, I couldn't even utter it.

"That's okay. I don't mind," I said as I not-so-subtly moved the inner part of my jacket, revealing slight cleavage. "I won't tell her if you don't."

James's eyes bulged like a couple of tennis balls as he stared at my tits. It was at that moment that I knew I had him. So much for his loyalty to his girlfriend. A pair of pert tits and a few kind words and he was already breathlessly running to grab a pen and piece of paper to write his phone number down, all the while shoving customers and coworkers alike out of the way.

He came back a minute later, huffing and puffing with a piece of grease-stained paper in his hands. He gave it to me and flashed a grin that revealed yellow, crooked teeth. I had the terrible luck of catching a whiff of his bad breath even if it was just for a moment.

I called him right then (from a burner phone, mind you, because there's no way I'd want to be traced back to this loser later on) just to make sure the number was right. I didn't think he would give me a wrong number, but I thought that maybe, in all that excitement, he simply messed up a digit, so I needed to be sure.

Once I was sure that it was his phone ringing, I hung up, winked at him, and told him I'd be looking forward to repaying him while turning around to leave with my bag of apples.

I ended up not buying anything except the apples, and once I was near the closest trash can, I tossed the bag inside. There was no way I'd touch those germ-infested apples that that ogre had hand-picked for me.

You know how I said I needed a shower after Robert? Well, just being so close to James Carter brought that feeling back tenfold. I ended up scrubbing myself so hard that night that the skin on my arms and legs was all red.

Just the reminiscence of interacting with James made me want to start scrubbing myself all over again, but I had to keep my goal in mind. He was an animal torturer, and he needed to pay for killing those innocent creatures.

Not even three hours after leaving Trader Joe's, I received a message from James Carter.

Feel Free To Scream

8

SWORDMASTER

He really was needy as hell, just as I initially assumed. The message he had sent me was riddled with typos, spelling errors, and a bunch of emojis constructed from symbols. I'd only ever seen Japanese business partners using them in creative ways—like making a smiley that looked like it was drinking beer or high-fiving someone—and I hated the fact that I'd never be able to look at them the same way again.

Chatting with James felt like chatting with an adult with a disability. He was a lot more talkative over text than he was in person. I kind of expected that, so I wasn't surprised.

We exchanged a dozen or so messages and got to know each other, and when I say we got to know each other, I really mean that it was mostly him talking about his love for anime, video games, and the Japanese culture.

Yup, he definitely fit the fedora-guy stereotype. I figured that I didn't even need to ask if he had a collection of action figures from his favorite comics and overpriced katanas that he used to hone his sword-fighting skills by slicing bottles of Mountain Dew.

He did show vague interest in me by asking me what I did for work and what my hobbies were, but then he quickly hijacked the topic by talking about himself. He also got a little too salacious early on, and I had no intention of taking another bath, so I told him to "be patient until our date smiley face."

As expected, he was pushy about when we should meet. Just out of curiosity, I asked about his girlfriend and whether she would suspect something. He replied that she was napping right next to him and didn't know a thing; plus that she was too dumb to figure it out.

So not only an animal torturer but also a cheater. In my mind, the moment he started undressing me with his eyes in Trader Joe's was the moment he cheated on his girlfriend.

Did I feel bad about wrecking the poor girl's relationship with this doofus? Absolutely not. In fact, I was doing her a favor. If it wasn't me, then it would have been some other woman.

Who am I kidding? No other woman would go out of her way to hook up with someone like James Carter. I know that everything I'm saying about him makes me look like a terrible, judgmental human being, and maybe I am. But at least, I'm not an animal torturer.

Besides, if this girl knew what James Carter was like and still chose to stay with him, that said a lot about her.

The next few days were somewhat agonizing. With the extra work at the company and the side-gig of being a justice hitman, I was exhausted. What mostly took up my energy was having to respond to James's messages.

He was incessant and constantly showered me with attention I never asked for. It was actually him who wanted the attention, and whenever I didn't respond for more than an hour, I was bombarded with tons of messages like *hello*, *are you there*, and multiple question marks.

Two days after exchanging numbers, I had a particularly busy day at work and hadn't managed to respond to him for a few hours. When I got back to the phone, I saw a bunch of messages that sounded something like this:

Why aren't you responding?
Why are you ignoring me?
Do you not like me anymore?
If you want me to leave you alone, just say so.
Please don't ignore me, baby. I'm worried about you.

It's really not that hard to send one message.
You're with someone else right now, aren't you?
I knew you were like all the other girls.
You whore.

No phone calls, though. Any normal person would have seen the red flags here and run as far as their legs could take them. I had seen the red flags even before meeting up with him, so these messages, although somewhat surprising, didn't deter me from completing my goal.

I politely explained how I was busy with work and listened to him ranting about how inconsiderate I was for not answering him for hours while he repeatedly paused his favorite anime and checked his phone for notifications from me.

He was already acting like a jealous boyfriend, even though we weren't in a relationship. I wrinkled my nose at the thought of anyone seeing our messages and thinking there was something between us.

Each message James sent me only revealed more and more about his insecurities, but it also swelled my wish to kill him. I didn't even care about him torturing animals anymore. I just wanted him dead so he could shut the hell up.

He was not only a terrible human being. He was also annoying as hell and absolutely boring.

I grew tired of listening to how he was learning Japanese and was one day going to move to Japan and become a famous manga artist. I rolled my eyes whenever he paraphrased a cringey quote from his favorite anime characters about protecting the weak or training to become strong or whatever it is that anime characters care about.

I honestly couldn't wait to get this over with. I was looking forward to the kill, but not to everything that would come before that. I didn't want to spend another minute

Feel Free To Scream

pretending to care about this man-child just so I could lure him into my trap, and yet, I knew it had to be done.

I reminded myself to be patient while I continued to gather info from him. I steered the topic toward pets and animals, and James easily fell into my trap. At first, he didn't open too much about it, stating that he was indifferent about animals.

I gently prodded, and he opened up, inch by inch. Apparently, when he was a kid, the family cat had scratched him, and then later, a stray dog had bitten him, so he remarked multiple times how unpredictable and dangerous those animals could be.

He didn't mention anything about torturing animals, but I read between the lines and noticed his contempt toward the creatures.

Whenever you ask someone enough questions about a topic, you'll start to get an idea of how they feel about it, even if they previously swore they are indifferent. That's what it was like with James, only, in his case, it immediately became apparent that the topic of animals was an elephant he was trying to hide (pun intended) because he knew society didn't condone such behavior.

I pressed a little more by lying how I found dogs disgusting and hated being around them. It's a pretty old but useful trick—if you can't get someone to open up, you open about something, and that will cause them to feel more comfortable about sharing their secrets with you.

With James, that was even easier than I imagined it would be. One or two messages from me saying something negative about cats and dogs and how they deserve to be tortured, and his tongue (or, in this case, fingers) unrolled and he was openly telling me about his adventures torturing and killing animals on the street.

He went into graphic details, and I'm afraid to say that some of those messages traumatized me. You know how there are people who are totally okay with slashers and seeing people die in all sorts of gruesome ways, but even the sight of a dog in a horror movie makes them turn their heads away because they're afraid the animal will die?

Well, that's me.

There's almost nothing that disgusts and pisses me off more than animal cruelty. That's why I wanted James Carter out of this world so badly. I had intended on going out on a date with him as soon as I confirmed he had really done what he did to the animals, and now that I had a confession from him, I didn't need to wait any longer.

The normal thing to do in this case would be going to the police and showing them the messages, but as I've witnessed firsthand, the justice system was flawed, and I couldn't risk losing the upper hand just so this animal torturer could get a maximum of two years in prison and then be back on the streets again.

Take matters into your own hands.

I couldn't wait any longer and suggested we go out the next night in search of some animals to "experiment" on. James seemed reluctant at first, but a simple "we can maybe go back to my apartment—winking smiley face" was enough to convince him.

I was going to bring a knife, but then he made my day by sending *I'll bring my katanas*. I told him how excited I was to try it out, and it was the truth. I had never held a real sword in my hands, and I wondered how easily it would cut through human flesh.

I finished work earlier the following day and told everyone at the company that I didn't care what kind of an emergency they would have because I'd be taking the rest of the day off completely—which meant I wouldn't answer any work emails or anything like that.

I took a twenty-minute nap in the afternoon, which was the time I probably would have taken to prepare for my date had this been a real date. I woke up fresh and perky, and even Summer the Red Riding Hood noticed it. I told her I was feeling full of energy and was therefore going to go out jogging.

She almost ruined my plan by asking if she could come along, but I told her I wanted to go alone and listen to a podcast; plus, she wouldn't be able to keep up with my pace. She didn't seem too bummed out by my stern decision.

I put on my leather jacket and gloves and walked to the location where James and I agreed to meet up. He didn't have a car and asked if I could pick him up, but since it wasn't too far away, I figured walking would be better (both in regards to calorie-burning and evidence-concealing).

I had kind of hoped that James would at least take a bath and dress up nicely for the "date," but one look at his dirty jacket and oversized trousers was enough for me to have my answer. When he turned to face me, I saw that he wore a bandana with some kind of symbol over his forehead.

I knew it was from an anime, but I couldn't tell which one because I never watched that stuff. My eyes fell on the two long sticks in his hand, and that's what got my heart racing.

When he met me for our *date*, his facial expression contorted into something that made him look like he was constipated. It was the same kind of expression he had back at Trader Joe's. He muttered a feeble "hi" when he saw me, which completely contrasted his chatty alter ego in his messages.

"Hey, handsome," I said.

He giggled like an embarrassed schoolgirl at that. I wondered if I went overboard with that comment and that he would see through my ruse, but then remembered that if he was stupid enough to believe I was interested in him, he would be stupid enough to believe an otherwise unbelievable compliment.

"My, what long swords you have," I said as my eyes shifted toward the sheathed katanas in his hand.

"You like them?" he asked as he presented both. "Here, you can have this one."

Both were similar, but I assumed that James had called dibs on the better one for himself. The sword felt light in my hand. I expected something made out of steel to be difficult to swing, but as soon as I unsheathed the blade and held it out in front of myself, I could tell how lightweight it was.

"Is this the real thing?" I asked as I gently touched the sharp edge of the blade.

It certainly felt sharp. I so badly wanted to slice James up right then.

"Of course it is," James said with an offended timbre. "I only buy the best qualities."

I swung the sword in the air a few times, producing a *swish-swoosh* before sheathing it.

"This sword is the best sword ever made," James proudly proclaimed with a slight bow. "They were originally used by the samurai, but thanks to the grace bestowed upon me by the gods, I was able to acquire them to hone my skills."

By "grace of the gods," I assume he meant allowance from his parents, which he then used to buy the cheapest versions off eBay. The swords were obviously of great importance to him, so I would leave them to him once everything was done. Not a good idea to hold on to a murder weapon, anyway.

"You train with these, huh?" I asked. "You must be really good."

I was screwing with him, but I did it in such a subtle way that he thought I was serious.

"Indeed," he replied. "I wake up early every morning and go outside for thirty minutes of meditating and sword training. But I only train to do good. I would never want to abuse the strength I have attained."

My grimace must have been that of sucking on sour candy. His body definitely didn't look like it reflected that power. Perhaps the thirty minutes of pretend-playing *Dragonball* in the backyard weren't enough to negate all the damage of sitting in front of his computer and eating Doritos.

If only you could attain the power to take a shower and buy some deodorant.

"Cool. So, let's go look for some animals, huh?" I grinned, no longer able to listen to how much he enjoyed the sound of his own voice. "There should be some in the alleys."

"Yes. Let us rid the world of this vermin," he exclaimed theatrically, undoubtedly a quote from anime because there was no way he could create a sentence like that one on his own.

He flashed me an emotional smile. I had to turn away from him and roll my eyes in such a wide circle that they hurt. I strode toward one of the alleyways and listened as his lumbering footsteps followed me.

James was pretty much out of breath even before we reached the first alley. Despite his inability to walk even a short distance without getting winded, he proceeded to spew nonsense about using *ki* to sense the "evil creatures' presence."

A few of his remarks actually made me believe that he was joking. There was no way anyone, especially not an adult in his late twenties, could say the things they said and believe in them.

But whenever I doubted whether he believed his own words, one look at his rigid face and eyes fervently scanning the alleys with the sword held firmly at the ready was enough to convince me otherwise.

I hadn't been looking for animals, of course. I had been trying to determine which alley was the least likely one to be checked any time soon. We spent ten or so minutes walking in circles. I already knew the area well and was acquainted with where the security cameras were, so I convinced James to avoid those areas.

The last thing I needed was for the police to review the camera footage and find me walking around with this wannabe-Goku.

We had made it to a particularly isolated alley, which I decided was perfect for murder. Alcoves and trash containers provided perfect cover, and the adjacent streets were rarely occupied.

I felt excitement surging in me. I unsheathed my sword and turned to face James. Just the thought of skewering his round belly with the katana made delectable shivers run down my spine.

He was oblivious to my voracious stare and instead focused on the corners of the alley, scanning them perhaps for any sleeping animals.

And then I heard it.

A soft mewl came from somewhere nearby and stopped the pleasant sensation on my skin. I turned toward the source of the sound and saw a tiny creature bathed in orange light, sauntering out of the shadow.

The tabby kitten's jaw opened, and she let out a baby-like mewl as she stared up at me and then at James. It bravely walked up to me and circled around my ankles, its soft fur gently caressing my skin.

It took everything in me not to let out a petulant "aww" and bend down to stroke her. I couldn't do it just yet. Not in front of James Carter. The kitten was entirely comfortable around me. It ran its cheek and side against my ankles, purring like a tractor so loudly that I could feel the vibrations through the touch.

Feel Free To Scream

"There it is. The spawn from hell," James exclaimed. "Stand back, my princess. I'll save you."

"Wait, what are you doing? That's just a baby," I said. "Her mom probably left to catch something to feed her."

The kitten stepped away from me, its warm fur gone and giving way for the cold air to envelop the exposed skin around my ankles. It approached James, but as if sensing he would not appreciate the same gesture, it sat on the ground and mewled up at him.

"It's still a baby, yes," James said. "But one day, it will become a monster just like all the others. It must be killed before that happens."

James white-knuckled the handle of his katana with both hands and raised it high above his head. I swear I could smell the sealed redolence under his armpits enveloping the air and reaching my nose.

The kitten continued staring up at James, mewling, oblivious to the evil man's intentions. I wanted to spend another few minutes making sure the alley was indeed safe, but I also had no intention of letting this monster harm such an innocent little creature.

My own speed surprised me.

James's face contorted into a hateful scowl, but before he could bring the blade down on the kitten, I had already unsheathed my katana and thrust it forward. For a moment, everything seemed to freeze while my brain belatedly processed what was going on.

It was as if the lights had been off and then someone turned them on the moment I blinked. The katana that I held was embedded in James's stomach all the way to the hilt. His scowl was gone and was instead replaced by a perplexed stare. His lip quivered as his eyes gravitated toward his abdomen where an ever-growing circle of blood expanded. He looked like he didn't understand why a hilt was sticking out of his stomach.

As if registering it too late, the sword slipped from his fingers and clattered to the ground. The noise was deafening in the emptiness of the alley. James's arms lowered, and he stumbled backward. I had let go of the hilt by then and watched as he grabbed at it, his face now fixed on me.

For a moment, I was sure that he was going to pull the sword out of his chest with some inhuman power and strike me. Instead, I heard a distinct *pffft* like a deflating balloon as he let out a wet fart. He stumbled backward and collapsed into a sitting position against the wall.

The kitten's meowing came more rapid and frequent, and my first thought was *oh shit, it's hurt*. But then I looked down and noticed that it was by the opposite wall, its back arched and its fur standing straight in fear.

Relief flooded me, followed by another thought that said *oh shit, I'm missing the best part*.

I approached James and got down on one knee, watching him as his chest rose and fell in rapid motions. His head turned toward me, and he coughed. A trickle of blood ran down his lip. He was already pale as spoiled milk.

I hadn't realized until then that a smile was fixed on my face. The pleasant sensation that prickled my skin was back, and now it went deeper and stronger like when you first enter a tub full of hot water and feel your entire body relaxing.

James opened his mouth and said a word, but I didn't understand him.

"Wh-why?" he repeated and then coughed again.

I looked down at the sword sticking from his belly. Blood dripped from the wound onto his pants and down on the floor where it collected in a puddle. Aside from his own body odor, a distinct smell of piss permeated the air.

"*Why?*" I raised my eyebrows. "You seriously have the audacity to ask me that? With all the shit you've done?"

But the blank stare on his face told me that he, indeed, had no idea why I had done it. I shook my head and decided to tell him, not because I thought he should know but because I wanted to watch the fear in his eyes as his life slipped from him.

"You torture animals. You were going to kill a cute, innocent kitten. What kind of a human does that? You had to know you'd pay for your crimes sooner or later, right? Or maybe you thought you could get away with it?"

James's breathing slowed. He coughed and then squeezed his eyes shut and made a painful facial expression. He looked at me again and swallowed. He looked like he wanted to say something but was gathering the strength to do so.

Please don't die just yet. Let me enjoy your suffering a little longer, I remember thinking to myself.

I practically didn't know what to do with myself from the immense pleasurable feeling that pervaded my body. I felt like I could run for miles, like I could jump twenty feet high, like I could tear walls and buildings down, like I could rip my own clothes into shreds just from the pure strength I possessed in that moment...

James asked something in a weak whisper, and it took me a moment to understand the question.

"You... You never li-liked me?"

I let out a hysterical guffaw. I felt like I could fall sideways on the floor and laugh until tears blurred my vision.

"Liked you?" I asked. "Please. Don't kid yourself. I mean, just look at you. Then look at me. Now look at you again. You see my point, right? You didn't seriously think you stood a chance with a woman like me, did you?"

I had to stop in order to laugh again.

When I was done, I cleared my throat and said, "I'm a beautiful, smart, and successful businesswoman with a bright future and lines of men just waiting to take me out.

And you're... well, you. To be honest, I'm impressed you even managed to find a girlfriend who's willing to be with you despite all your flaws. Good job on that." I gave him a thumbs up. "Shows that you're willing to get out of your comfort zone. Not that it matters anymore since you'll be dead soon."

Humiliating him like this turned me on. I hadn't realized that until the vibrating sensation between my legs became unbearable. I never understood those men who liked being humiliated and dominated by women in sex, but now that I was standing above this dying man, I realized that it was yet another kink I should add to my list.

I watched as the corners of James's eyebrows upturned and his lips and cheek trembled. Soft whimpering sounds came from his mouth, and I thought I distinctly heard him calling to his mom.

"Oh, at least die with dignity, you loser. Those animals had feelings, too, you know? You're not that special," I said with complacency.

He repeated something that sounded like "please" in quick succession, and then everything stopped. His speaking, his chest heaving up and down, the trembling of his lips that brought me such immense joy...

Just like that, James Carter was dead.

Shit. That was too quick, I thought to myself, once again having that feeling of almost reaching a climax and then getting interrupted. James Carter had caused immense pain to animals, and now he was dead too soon. He didn't suffer enough.

I knew that I would need to practice in order to prolong my victims' suffering. As I stood up, I took a moment to enjoy the scenery. James's head was slumped forward, further accentuating his triple chins. His face was drained of color, and the trickle of blood that had come out of his mouth was already dry on his chin(s). The katana that he admired so much stuck out of his enormous, round belly, and an abundance of blood covered his clothes below.

It was the most beautiful sight I had ever seen.

I admired it just as an artist would admire his painting on a canvas. God, I wanted to take pictures so badly. I wanted to freeze this moment forever, but unfortunately, photographic memory would have to do.

The incessant mewling broke me out of my trance. I turned around to see the kitten still stuck by the wall, staring at me with caution.

"It's all right, baby. You're okay," I said as I slowly approached her.

She didn't try running. I squatted down and petted the kitten. It mewled defiantly some more and then relaxed under my touch, its crying weakening until it completely stopped.

"Go on. Back to your home," I said. "And not a word to anyone, yeah?"

I grinned and stood up. I looked at James's body one last time and bit my lower lip.

It physically took me a lot of effort to pry my gaze away from the magnificent sight and stroll out of the alley.

9

PUBLICITY

James Carter's death held a special place in my heart. Whenever I could grab a quiet moment alone, I closed my eyes and reminisced the whole thing. It was short, but that was okay.

It reminded me a lot of when I lost my virginity to my high-school crush, Daniel Lewis. We had been eyeing each other for a long time, and then one day, he asked me out on a date. The whole school knew that we liked each other and it was pretty much only a matter of time until he asked me out.

Hell, I would have taken the preemptive step, but I didn't want any rumors about me to circulate the school. Daniel and I ended up dating for about eight months, and I slept with him half a year into our relationship.

I was madly in love with him, and that's what caused my first sex to be so intense. It was slow, it was passionate, and it was forming a connection with Daniel on a deeper level (no pun intended).

For a week after our first time, I found my mind wandering toward the intercourse. I wanted to keep it in my memory forever, but just like with all things, it soon faded. I read somewhere once that when we remember something, we actually remember the last time we remembered it, and that's why it fades from our memory.

Daniel and I had made love many more times before I realized I no longer loved him and broke up with him. I have no idea how the sudden transition occurred; it just did. One moment, I was willing to give my life for him, and in the next, sleeping with him felt like a chore.

He was devastated. We were at the park when I dumped him, and he cried like a river. I wanted to go, but I also didn't want to be rude and just dump him and leave. Truthfully, I felt embarrassed by the stares of the passersby.

I saw Daniel in school here and there after that, but we never even said hi to each other. I knew for a fact that he was devastated, and I felt bad for leaving him the way I did, but I couldn't stay with him just because I wanted to avoid hurting his feelings, right?

Either way, I also learned things in that relationship, especially things about myself: like that it takes me a long time to get attached to someone, but my emotions quickly become extinguished; and that I don't like it when I feel vastly superior to a partner, etc.

I would later learn that Daniel Lewis got engaged with, and later married, my high-school classmate Ann Edwards. They have two children now, and one of them has my name, which I learned from a Facebook post. Yikes. Guess some people never move on.

When I returned home the night I killed James Carter, Summer was in the kitchen, waiting for the microwave to heat the frozen pizza. She remarked something about me being back so soon from my jogging, and then I suddenly realized *oh crap, I forgot I told her I was going jogging.* I told her that I didn't want to overdo it because it was a little cold, and she didn't ask another question.

For a moment, I wondered if I could actually kill someone right in front of her and then think of an excuse that would clear me of suspicions. *No, no, I didn't kill him. I, uh, I found him like this in the apartment. Oh, the knife? It's to, uh, cut any tight clothes on him and improve blood circulation, you know?*

I took a long bath again, not because I felt like I needed to get the blood off but because I could still smell James

Carter's bodily odor on my skin and clothes (I also later took those clothes to the dry cleaner's.)

Taking a bath after killing had become a ritual for me, just like drinking coffee as soon as I woke up. I imagined a world where I wouldn't need to hide the fact that I killed someone.

I would return home. Summer would have a couple of questions, but I would simply raise my palm to silence her, which would mean *we'll talk after my bath.* Or maybe she'd even run the bath for me (*Hey, sis, I know you must be tired from stabbing that thief with an ice pick, so I went ahead and made you a bubble bath*) so when I got back home, I could plop inside without a worry in the world.

I diligently checked the news for the next few days, mostly focusing on the criminal activity and arrests section. It was less than a day after James's death that the news with the headline NOTORIOUS MAN WHO TORTURED ANIMALS FOUND DEAD came out.

It was on the front pages of *The Oregonian*.

The media descriptively mentioned how Carter was found with his beloved sword in his gut—the same sword he used to butcher all those animals. I found it poetic that his own weapon had been his undoing.

Needless to say, the case garnered a ton of attention. The only people who mourned Carter's death were his mother and his girlfriend Vanessa. I remember that the news article quoted Vanessa. She said something along the line of *He was my reason for living. I don't know what I'm going to do without him.*

You're going to go out and find someone who's not willing to cheat on you with a pretty face, sister. You can find yourself a James Carter in any trash can or sewer you peek into, so it shouldn't be hard to replace him.

The community of animal rights activists openly rejoiced at the news. They even posted a picture of James (an unflattering one, but then again, all of his pics were like that) on their website and Twitter with the caption "Someone succeeded where the American justice system failed. Karma is a bitch, James."

Now, I didn't really think about gaining any publicity when I first started doing this, but I have to say that scrolling through the comments gave me a warm feeling inside.

Although many of the people wrote lengthy "holier than thou" comments about how they didn't condone any witch hunts and vigilante justice, the majority was generally supportive of my action. Comments like *the killer is a hero* and *this is how it should be done* stood out for the most part, but the one that brought my attention was someone calling me *Animal Protector.*

I liked that title. It went well with my name. Not that I could plaster it on my LinkedIn profile or anything like that, though. I noticed a ton of deleted comments as well, which I assumed were supportive of the vigilante murderer.

Portland police released a statement later that day, identifying that the perpetrator was still at large (wow, what a shock!) and that they had no suspects. Their assumption was that James got into an altercation with someone and things escalated, and that worked well in my favor because it meant they weren't able to connect any of the murders yet.

The support I received from the public only further strengthened my resolve. I was determined to make the world a better place by eliminating the scumbags that plagued it, one person at a time.

I didn't draw the line at animals, though.

Nope. As much as I love animals, I'm the kind of person who can empathize more with the pain of humans, especially the pain of children.

88

My next victim was a man working as a VP for a video gaming company. Jeff Lee had been accused of pedophilia during a sting by a famous YouTube channel. The YouTuber in question pretended to be a fourteen-year-old boy online, and according to the official story, the VP sent inappropriate pictures and engaged in sexual conversations.

In the video filmed by the YouTuber, we can see the VP opening the door in a T-shirt with his company's logo (great marketing right there) before quickly closing it, ignoring the cameraman's shouts and insults.

Even that video evidence yielded no results; the VP didn't get terminated from his job nor arrested and prosecuted. It was another one of those "innocent until proven guilty" situations.

The problem is the "until" part can last forever, and I was not a very patient woman. That's why I never saw the charm in playing cards. Jeff Lee was an even easier target than James Carter.

He obviously didn't learn his lesson from the first sting because all I had to do was create an account on a shady website and send him a message pretending I was a young boy (I didn't know if he strictly liked just one gender, so I wanted to play it safe.)

By the time he answered, I had already received messages from five other adults showing interest in meeting up. I felt like a kid in a toy shop. All these victims at my disposal to choose from!

But I set my priorities straight. Jeff Lee would be my first one. Plus, I couldn't go on a killing spree, massacring all these pedophiles (as much as I wanted to) because the police would have no problem narrowing down the list of suspects.

Once Jeff Lee answered my message, we agreed to meet up at his place.

Feel Free To Scream

Before meeting up, I drove around his neighborhood a few times, checking out his place. No security cameras; not even alarm systems. What an idiot. Then again, if he had a lot of young boys coming to his house, he probably wanted to avoid keeping any evidence, so maybe not an idiot after all.

Then again, he gave his home address to someone online—something kids were taught by their parents not to do, so an idiot after all.

When the door opened, I was greeted by a middle-aged man with grizzled hair and thick glasses. The sight of me visibly confused him, and I flashed him the friendliest smile I could muster, even though I could feel the anger-induced vein dancing on my forehead. I gritted my teeth and presented myself to the VP as a cute and flirtatious stranger, which was something I often used whenever I talked to customer support.

The only time my feminine charm didn't work on men was when they were either gay or asexual. Even the ones who were happily married or in relationships liked having a beautiful woman talking to them and showing visible signs of liking them.

My charm didn't work on Jeff, which only confirmed for me that he wasn't into women.

After a brief exchange where he asked me who I was and what I wanted, he tried to slam the door shut in my face. I was prepared for that outcome, so my hand was already in my handbag, the forefinger on top of the pepper spray.

The brown liquid caught his eyes by surprise, and by the time he put his hands up in front of him, it was already too late. Jeff screamed and stumbled backward where he smashed his head into the wall.

It was so loud that I thought he had just died without me even touching him. But then he moved again; crawled around the foyer with eyes firmly squeezed shut. Just like with MacGuffin, I let myself inside, observed the street, and then closed the door to give us some privacy.

I wanted to try out something new this time, and that's why I used the pepper spray. With Jeff blinded and unable to fight back, I was able to do with him whatever I pleased.

One thing I learned from my James Carter kill was that talking to the victim and telling them what awaited them grew their fear. I wanted to see what Jeff Lee's breaking point was, so I didn't do anything to him just yet.

Instead, I gently spoke to him.

I told him how I was going to kill him slowly and how nobody was going to hear him scream. I told him how his wife and two daughters would return home from their visit with the in-laws to find his rotting corpse splayed inside the house. I told him what creative tools I had at my disposal for slicing, breaking, drilling, cutting, ripping, tearing, etc.

That last one was a lie, but I enjoyed instilling fear in the fucker.

After resisting and blindly knocking over some objects in the house, Jeff stopped fighting and instead pleaded. I made it a point to take slow steps around the room, causing him to constantly whip his head in the direction of the sound, wincing whenever my fingers brushed his back and hair.

He was utterly at my mercy.

This was it. This is what I'd been looking for this whole time. That feeling of power—the knowledge that I held this person's worthless life in my hands and that I had the ability to snuff it out on a whim.

The pleasure I felt then was so powerful that I felt like I needed a bucket of cold water to come to my senses. The emotions clouded my judgment, carried me away. It would be so easy to make fatal mistakes in those moments. One moment of carelessness and I would leave a trail for the police to find me.

But I was better than that.

Also, remember how I mentioned that I'm not too patient? Well, Jeff Lee helped me realize that my impatience bled into other aspects of my life. For example, just ten or so minutes of listening to Jeff beg for his pathetic life lost its effect on me, and I found myself suppressing the urge to yawn.

Jeff offered me money to spare his life, but that wasn't why I was there. When I glanced at my watch, I realized that it was getting late, and I still had a presentation to prepare for tomorrow morning.

I walked up behind Jeff, yanked his head back by the hair, and sliced his throat with a knife. He produced similar gurgling sounds to Robert, only a lot louder. Blood sprayed out of his neck in such large quantities that I had to backstep to avoid getting it on my clothes.

I knew there were probably some microscopic particles that had still made it on my favorite Doc Martens and that they would need thorough cleaning later. Actually, I would probably need to get rid of the shoes because the forensics would find shoeprints in the pedophile's house.

Such a shame. I really liked those shoes.

By the time I looked up from my footwear, Jeff was already motionless on the ground in an ever-expanding pool of dark liquid.

Blood had sprayed everywhere, and I figured that the crew responsible for cleaning a crime scene was going to have a lot of work. Sorry, guys, but a job is a job.

The puddle was so big that I had to jump over it. I let myself out of the house, all the while whistling the tune of *God of justice* by Tim Hughes. As always, when I returned home, I took a long bath.

The media went wild by the end of the weekend. Jeff Lee's face was on every major news website along with a mass deletion of comments, blogs, and videos supporting the killer they dubbed *Portland Executioner*.

I didn't like the executioner part, but oh, well. It felt good being unique in something.

The police said nothing about the connection of the two recent murders, which led me to believe that they didn't yet know that they were correlated, but the public already speculated who the Executioner's victims were (and that included victims who I never even knew about), and then the information was impossible to stop.

I was indignant with the legal system, to be honest. Here I was doing the world a favor and I had to hide like a common criminal. In fact, if they caught me, I knew I'd be tried as nothing more than a murderer and sentenced to a couple hundred years in prison.

Sure, the people would probably be pissed – most of them, anyway. Sure, they'd call me a hero, and I would probably get a tribute video on YouTube and receive tons of fan mail while in prison, but that wouldn't make the world a better place.

As much as I liked this anonymous online attention, it wasn't my priority. I didn't want a red carpet rolled out in front of me and paparazzi stalking me everywhere to take pictures for their *Portland Executioner shows off her toned arms in a sleeveless shirt* articles that would get a dozen clicks (Not that it would be a thing anyway, as appealing as it sounds. At least, not until they regulate the law and allow regular citizens to lynch criminals).

What I wanted was to create a safe environment for the people, just as it was intended to be. I figured that I wouldn't need to kill every single criminal on this planet, as much as I wanted to. I just needed to continue at this pace, and the news about the Portland Executioner would spread enough to drive fear into anyone who thought about engaging in criminal activity.

I spent days reveling in the news and the memes about the Executioner that flooded the internet. I honestly felt like a celebrity. Even though no one knew who I really was, they knew what I was doing, and they loved me for it. That somehow made it even more magical.

They didn't like me because of my looks. I wasn't like the Kardashians in the sense that I released a sex tape and became famous despite having no talent. No, what I was doing was art, but it was also making the world a better place.

I didn't waste my time finding my next victim.

A young man living in San Francisco was next on my list. I hadn't even considered going out of town to kill anyone, but I had a one-week-long business trip there, so I figured I might as well kill some time (and criminals).

Going sightseeing? Posting on Instagram the same picture of the Golden Gate Bridge that every person and their mother posted whenever they visited? Nah. I'd been to SF more times than I could count, and I didn't feel like there was anything else left for me to see.

There was, however, stuff for me to do with my newfound hobby.

The victim in question was a twenty-something-year-old dude from Serbia called Andrej who was involved in a hit and run that resulted in the death of a fifteen-year-old girl.

Since Andrej was the son of a prominent TV channel CEO, his daddy managed to pull some strings and get the perpetrator convicted to eight months of house arrest – just enough to give to the raging public a crumb to calm them down.

I read the news of the incident in detail. The girl who died, Sophie, was a talented musician who volunteered during the weekends. After going above the speed limit, Andrej hit her while she was on the pedestrians' cross and, after a moment of hesitation, drove off.

Sophie was still alive at that time, so if he had called an ambulance, she might have lived. It took several years to even bring the case to court, and by the time Andrej finally was sentenced to the meager punishment that I don't think was even worth mentioning, the public pretty much forgot all about Sophie.

The victim's family still remembered, though. The parents and the little brother who cried in front of live cameras on every anniversary of Sophie's death felt old wounds reopening.

Meanwhile, Andrej was living a happy life: driving expensive cars, going out to fancy restaurants, and splurging on his dad's money. It was pretty much a public secret that the people had turned a blind eye to.

The evidence was in the open, and yet, for some reason, a criminal didn't get convicted *properly*. When I was younger, I believed that there was no way anyone could escape the law; at least not in America. I heard from many of my foreign third-world-country friends that you could get away with almost any crime outside the US borders if you had enough money to bribe the officials.

They went into extensive details about the rich elite paying to have their crimes erased even though everyone knew about them. But that was outside America, and things like that didn't happen here.

That was, at least, what I thought until I learned that we're just better at cleaning up after ourselves.

You'd think that Andrej would be well protected. I imagined a couple of seven-foot-tall bodyguards risking their lives for low pay to protect the son of the man who was paying them. I probably wasn't the only one who wanted a piece of him.

Luckily for me, Andrej was not a mob boss who could afford to have meagerly-dressed skanks and expensive bodyguards who wore sunglasses and earbuds around him. It was his dad's money after all.

I learned that Andrej lived in an expensive condo where security was pretty much impregnable, so taking him out there would be out of the question. I mean, I could kill him there, but I'd be caught right after.

I also learned that there were certain restaurants, cafés, and clubs that he went out to. Multiple reports had been made about him getting drunk and harassing female guests by sitting at their tables and hitting on them.

You can see where I'm going with this.

One night, I went out to Arabian Nights, which was one of the destinations that Andrej zealously visited every week. I wore my black "dinner outfit" as I called it, along with a blonde wig and floral laced gloves, and sat alone at a table while drinking a martini.

The slow and tranquil jazz music was interrupted by a booming voice that spoke in a language that sounded very similar to Russian. Andrej walked into the restaurant, his shirt unbuttoned, his neck and hairy chest glistening with sweat.

He went on to hug and kiss the waiters on the cheek, telling them how they were his favorite waiters. The staff, visibly uncomfortable at his presence, directed him to a nearby table.

The atmosphere changed rather quickly. Not only were the nearby guests bothered by Andrej's overbearing attitude, but the staff was, too. Their facial expressions looked like they were fed up with this particular guest. I could imagine them scrambling to grab any other shift except the night when Andrej shows up.

The night went on while I slowly sipped, giving Andrej occasional glances. Our eyes met a few times, and as soon as he noticed me, he could not avert his gaze from me.

Feminine charm.

He was actually handsome, I had to notice. Too bad he was a piece of shit. Once I caught his attention, I averted my gaze and smiled cunningly to intrigue him further. Now, all I had to do was wait.

Sure enough, Andrej invited himself to my table soon, spewing drunken poems in accented English about how I was as pretty as the first flower in spring. Before I became the Executioner, I would have been uncomfortable to have a guy approach me like this, but knowing what I was going to do to him, I invited him to join me even though he was already seated across from me.

We made some small talk (By "we", I really mean me because he was not smart or sober enough to understand some of my subtle remarks.) When I stood up to leave, he grabbed me by the wrist and slurred something that was supposed to sound like "baby, where are you going?" but sounded like one long word instead.

I pulled a note out of my bra—his eyes bulged at that—and slipped it to him. It was a paper with the address of a motel where I'd be staying. I told him to come to the parking lot later that night at around midnight.

I, of course, didn't have a room in that motel. I deliberately chose a place that had no security cameras and invited Andrej to a secluded part behind the dumpsters where no one would see us.

By the time he arrived, I was freezing. He was twenty minutes late, and I honestly wanted to stab him in the face right then. He was even more drunk than in the restaurant, which worked to my advantage.

I lured him deeper into the darkness. He became a little too touchy. I squirmed, but I have to say that he was also really good with his hands. At one point, he caught me by surprise by putting a hand on my waist and reeling me closer to him. Before I could figure out how to react, our lips were pressed tightly together.

His tongue squirmed into my mouth, and the smell of booze wafted into my face. It felt like a frog wiggling in my mouth. As disgusting as it was, there was also something erotic about it. I gave in and pretended to relax while I kissed him back. He wasn't half as bad as I expected him to be, to be honest.

It wasn't the sexual aspect of the kissing that aroused me. It was what came next. I waited patiently and felt Andrej's body tensing up. He wanted me. Bad. Nothing else in the world mattered. I was sure that if I touched his crotch, I would feel a bulge there. His hand reached toward my breast.

With one slick motion, I reached into my purse, pulled out the taser, and pressed it against his crotch while pushing the button. Andrej's body convulsed violently. His facial expression morphed into various shapes as he fell on the ground.

He peered up at me with a look of confusion. He looked like he had completely sobered up. Seeing realization drape his face—the realization that he was so close to getting some and then had it yanked away from him in the last moment—was oh-so-satisfying.

"You bitch!" he shouted.

It came out as *beetch.* I zapped him again, not letting up this time. He looked like he was having an epileptic attack. I didn't want to waste too much time with this one. It was cold. The spot was not one hundred percent concealed, and I wanted to get some much-needed sleep before my meeting tomorrow.

I brought out a hammer from my purse. I was determined to break his body the way he broke that girl's when he hit her with the car.

"This is for Sophie, you sick fuck," I said as I brought the hammer down on his head.

10

COPYCAT

Things went on normally after that. I claimed multiple murders, and with each one, I got better. I read somewhere once that killing is something that becomes easier the more you do it. I didn't really believe it or even give it much thought before I'd become the Portland Executioner.

After the fifth kill, I had grown somewhat desensitized to the rush I felt with my victims. I learned to improve and prolong the fun. I enveloped them in fear and despair in their final moments and watched as the realization of what waited for them washed over their faces. I enjoyed the fear in their eyes as the last thing they saw in this twisted world was the face of their executioner.

But after every kill, I felt sort of empty, like waiting for a dessert that never came. I didn't know what it was that my kills were missing, but I was determined to continue experimenting until I found it.

Usually, I tried to kill the criminal the way their victims suffered. For example, there was an ex-convict who raped a young girl and then choked her to death, so I made it a point to use a long stick with splinters, and... well, you get the point. Anyway, I strangled him with a garrote wire in front of a mirror so he could see his own scared expression while his vision darkened.

Then there was the ex-military who shot a teenager in the back because he was dressed as a robber for Halloween and the soldier thought he was threatened for real. The judge accepted the jury's verdict that it was self-defense and dropped all charges on the ex-soldier. I ended up shooting nails from a nail gun into his vertebrae all the way up to the neck.

He was quadriplegic and begging for death before I killed him. I was honestly tempted to leave him like that. It certainly would be a worse punishment, letting him live like that rather than killing him, but I didn't want him talking, so he got one nail through the eye. It killed him instantly.

So, yeah. Experimenting.

After all, my victims were all murderers, rapists, robbers, and other scum that the world wouldn't miss, so using them as guinea pigs was okay. The public certainly didn't seem to mind. By then, the police had determined that the murderer was most likely a woman, which caused the news to spread even more.

More and more, on my walks through the city, instead of the *KEEP PORTLAND WEIRD* graffiti, I would see depictions of a woman with a sack on her head with one hole for an eye, a bloodstained apron, and a cleaver in her hand. The usual phrase above the murals said *COMMIT A CRIME. MAKE MY DAY.*

A fan page dedicated to me already existed on Facebook where the admins would make posts impersonating the Portland Executioner.

Just saw a guy on the bus with a MAGA cap. Guess who you'll see on the morning news tomorrow.

Although the page was satirical, I didn't appreciate them making posts that some of the boomers took way too seriously. News about the Portland Executioner already caused widespread panic with some people, and the page didn't help make it any better.

Although the public was generally supportive of the Executioner, some still thought the person needed to be brought to justice for going against the law and killing human beings.

Those frigging idiots.

I was doing the cops and the public a favor. They should have offered me a medal of honor for risking my life to keep the streets safe, and instead, they were labeling me a criminal.

I didn't let that dissuade me, though. I would just need to continue killing hardcore criminals and prove to the people that I was a doer of good. But since everyone had become so cautious, I had to be patient and bide my time. I wasn't worried because I knew that opportunity would come sooner rather than later.

With all the extra work I put in, I was starting to feel burnt out. I didn't even feel the symptoms until Summer mentioned how cranky I was one morning when I told her not to chew her cereal so loud. That's how suddenly burnout usually comes, right?

You work at full capacity, even put in extra time. You feel good. You feel great. You feel motivated. This lasts for a while, and then, one day, you just wake up feeling tired. The person who has the bad luck to be the first human of the day to interact with you annoys the hell out of you—even with the small, unconscious things they do like breathing.

Then you have the first meeting at work, and you wish you could strangle everyone because they're so slow. You can't wait for your lunch break so you can regenerate just a little bit. By the time you're done with work, you hate your job, your clients, your roommate, and your neighbor.

It's usually too late then. A lot of people can't afford to take long vacations or sick leaves, and even when they can, it's not enough time to unwind. Either that, or they don't know how to unwind effectively.

You know those people who go on vacation, but then they say something like, "I don't work. I only answer work emails"? Well, those are exactly the kinds of things that cause burnout to linger or progress to a higher stage.

Most of us suffer from stage one burnout, come to think of it. We just learn to ignore it because the change is so gradual we don't even see it, and if we do, we accept it as normal.

I know it's normal for the American working man to spend all day long at work until 6 p.m., only to have the few remaining hours to themselves, but I find that culture absolutely wild.

Sometimes I think about those things. Not too deeply, though, because they bum me out. Who wouldn't get depressed at the thought of working fifty hours a week for the next thirty-something years only to retire and have all the time in the world just a couple of years before death?

Anyway, I spent one weekend doing nothing but eating junk food and watching Netflix in my pajamas. I even slept until noon and skipped my jogging sessions and didn't feel guilty about it.

Even the Portland Executioner needs a break.

On Monday, I returned home to see Summer beaming with excitement. She was sitting on the couch, ramrod-straight, and staring at the show that ran on the TV. It wasn't a funny show, and yet, Summer had a smile on her face.

"What's the good news?" I asked as I dropped my handbag on the kitchen counter.

"I have a boyfriend," Summer exclaimed, somewhat shyly, somewhat proudly.

It caught me off guard, but I was pleasantly surprised. I knew that she'd gone out on a couple of dates here and there, but I didn't expect her to get serious about it because she mentioned a few times that she still had problems because of what Robert did to her.

"Wow," was all I managed to exclaim.

A flurry of questions poked my mind, and I didn't know which one to ask first. I didn't have to because Summer hopped up on her feet and started talking about her new boyfriend.

Words weren't necessary for me to understand how much she liked him. Maybe she liked him even a little too much. I wanted to warn her to slow down and not get her hopes up too much before she got to know him better, but I didn't want to be the grumpy person who always looks at things negatively.

Summer spoke rapidly, without a moment to take a breath, and among the torrent of words, the one thing I was able to understand was that the guy's name was Malik and that he worked as a barista at a nearby Starbucks.

Then, just like that, Summer's tongue stopped working, and the apartment was filled with silence as we stared at each other. It took my brain a moment to register the final sentence that she had uttered before going silent.

"Malik will be here in a bit."

"Like, today?" I asked.

"Yes."

"Here? In our apartment?"

"Uh-huh." Summer nodded.

"But I just got back home. I could go out to give you two time and all, but—"

"What? No! I'm not telling you this so you can leave. I invited him here so you could meet him."

"Oh," I uttered, dumbstruck.

I was both shocked and honored. My little sister was bringing her boyfriend to the apartment so I could give them my blessing. If you remember what I said about Summer at the beginning, it's that she always does things opposite of what everyone tells her. That's why I was so surprised that she wanted my approval for Malik.

Who knows, maybe the whole thing with Robert finally made her realize that the parents and I were right all along and wanted good for her. Not that I was happy about that because that's a terrible way to come to your senses.

Feel Free To Scream

I wish I could say I wasn't nervous about meeting my little sister's new boyfriend, but I was. In fact, the knot that tied in my stomach was oddly reminiscent of the one I felt after accidentally killing Robert. I hoped I wouldn't get too nervous and say something stupid in front of Malik.

Malik was a shy, handsome young man around Summer's age. He was so polite and courteous that I just wanted to pinch his cheeks and give him pet names. He called me "ma'am" until I told him that first-name basis was okay.

His occasional stuttering and visibly frightened body language made him look a little awkward, but that was okay. Compared to Robert, who waltzed in like he owned the place and put his feet up on the table for everyone to see the holes in his socks, I preferred someone shy like Malik.

It felt kind of weird sitting at the table with him and Summer because I felt like I had been given the role of an approving parent even though I never asked for it. Malik said no more than he was asked, and the entire time, he and Summer exchanged affectionate stares with each other.

At one point, since the TV was on, some news about the Portland Executioner came on. That's when Malik became more talkative. He knew a lot about the Executioner, and I mean *a lot*.

He was really interested in criminology and serial killers. The passionate way in which he spoke about the Portland Executioner had both Summer and me staring at him in awe. He realized it, but not before spending a solid five minutes tirelessly talking about the murders with utter fascination in his voice.

"I find the Portland Executioner extremely fascinating," he exclaimed.

Once he saw Summer's and my gazes fixed on him, his face grew red, and he apologized.

I was honestly happy for Summer. It had been a while since I'd seen her so full of life. Come to think of it, the last time I saw her that happy was when she was still deludedly in love with Robert the Rapist.

That thought made me ogle Malik in a suspicious manner, but I decided that a polite man like him couldn't possibly be a dick like Robert.

"Now, we just need to find *you* a boyfriend, and then we can go on double dates," Summer said as she wrapped her arms around Malik.

I nervously chuckled at that.

Yeah, no. No way I'd be able to live that kind of life—working a full-time job, being the Executioner, and then having a boyfriend on top of that. Not that I planned on being alone for the rest of my life because I didn't. I just didn't feel like dating then.

I could already hear Aunt Mary's voice hounding me at the next family gathering.

Oh, but sweetheart, you're running out of time! No man will want to marry you after you're thirty. And, not to mention, you need time to give birth to children. With hips as beautiful as yours, it would be a shame not to have at least two miniature copies of yourself.

Sure thing, Aunt Mary. That's why you can't stand Uncle Harold and always talk about how you should have run off with that rich German who offered to marry you.

That was one thing I never understood. I'm not sure if it's just a family thing or if it's prevalent everywhere, but many of my relatives are in unhappy marriages because they got pregnant and then decided to stick together for the kids.

I can count at least five uncles and aunts who constantly pull me aside at family gatherings to give me advice not to get married. They always say it as a joke, but I can detect some truth hidden by the ironic remark.

Uncle Artie is the only one who doesn't hide his hate for marriage and makes it a point to let everyone know how he never wanted to have a child and only stayed with his wife because of it.

I mean, come on. I can understand if you're pro-life, but ever heard of Durex?

When it was time for Malik to leave, Summer said she was going out to say goodbye to him. It was already dark out, and I shot daggers at her silently, trying to convey telepathically that it was dangerous.

As it is with Red Riding Hood, she shrugged and asked, "What?" obliviously before Malik understood my intent. He promised to have her back within ten minutes. Such a nice guy.

Everything seemed to be going really well. I enjoyed the attention of being the Portland Executioner, Summer was finally happy, and the world was becoming a better place.

Then one morning, I woke up and read the breaking news that was so much in my face it obscured my entire vision.

PORTLAND EXECUTIONER STRIKES AGAIN. PREGNANT WOMAN FOUND DEAD AT HOME.

You know how you sometimes read one word wrong and it changes the entire context into something comical? That's what I thought happened to me here. In fact, I firmly *believed* that was the case, so I reread the headline a few more times.

When the words didn't change, I read them once more very slowly, letter by letter.

The article talked about a pregnant woman in her twenties who had been found dead at her home in Hawthorne. The body had been discovered that morning, and the police claimed she was killed no more than a week ago. There was a message written on paper next to the victim, supposedly a message from the Portland Executioner, daring the police to catch him.

The last victim I killed was a drug dealer in Gresham, and it was over two weeks ago. The closer I got to the bottom of the article with each read sentence, the more I felt something boiling inside me. It was a sort of insatiable, destructive feeling that I immediately likened to anger.

Summer had been right across from me, and we had been eating breakfast, so when she asked me what was wrong, I forced my muscles to relax. She became talkative about something, but I zoned out, my mind still focused on the article.

The response of the public was swift. The people who praised the Executioner as a protector and bringer of justice quickly rescinded that title, and it wasn't long until I was labeled a horrible criminal, fit only for the most gruesome kind of death penalty.

Cancel culture at its finest. Today you're a hero; tomorrow you wake up to find out you're a criminal.

I wanted to throw stuff and scream. How could they be so stupid and not see that this was a copycat killer? The Portland Executioner was a doer of good, not evil! I would never kill a pregnant woman unless she did something really bad!

I needed time to think, but I couldn't because of Summer's incessant babbling. I interrupted her chatter and told her I needed to leave for work earlier. On the way to the office, I was like a ticking bomb. The people on the street may have either realized it, or I got lucky because no one bumped into me, honked at me, catcalled, or anything like that.

I swear I was so pissed I could have thrown hot coffee in their face if that happened.

Before walking into the office, I took a moment to take a few deep breaths and compose myself. *Breathe in. Breathe out.* Just like the Israeli yoga instructor said.

It didn't help.

I effectively felt my cheek twitching from the suppressed anger as I smiled at my coworkers and made my way to my workspace. As the universe would always have it, whenever one thing goes bad, everything goes bad.

In my case, I had a ton of back-to-back meetings with people who asked questions that had already been resolved, causing the meetings to extend well beyond the designated time.

By the time I had lunch, I felt like I was pretty much ready to explode at the next person who came to me with a stupid question. The people in the cafeteria probably noticed my attitude because no one wanted to sit with me. Dario and a couple of others said hi but then distanced themselves from me with rapid steps.

I spent most of my lunch break scrolling through the news. The latest death of the Portland Executioner flooded every major news outlet. Already, a Facebook page called STOP THE PORTLAND EXECUTIONER had been erected. The profile picture was the mural of the butcher woman with the sack on her head crossed over in red.

On top of all the public backlash, the mayor had also given a statement that he would have police patrolling the streets in larger numbers, and if that didn't work, a curfew would be put into place.

I put my phone and fork down and rubbed my throbbing temples.

Breathe in. Breathe out. That's it, just do it slowly. Brea—

Oh, fuck that yoga instructor. Her breathing didn't help for shit. It was just a placebo, like praying. I needed some ibuprofen to stave off the migraine that pounded my head.

I knew that mulling over the copycat killer right now would do no good. I had to make a plan.

That's what I always did whenever I was faced with a dire situation. If I could resolve it right away, I would. But if I didn't have a solution the moment the incident occurred, I'd spend some time despairing or being angry, and then I'd make a plan to counter the situation.

If the police couldn't identify that this last murder was done by a fake Portland Executioner, then I would prove it to them.

Feel Free To Scream

11

SUBURBS

I ended up killing, not one but two criminals. One was a gynecologist who worked in her father's clinic and caused a miscarriage to a pregnant patient. She was sued, but nothing came of it.

I gutted her and yanked her intestines out as a magician would a string of rags from his sleeve. She screamed so loud before dying that my ears hurt.

The second victim was a gang member involved in a petty robbery. He ended up shooting a father of a then-four-year-old daughter who was in the car with him when it happened. He had served twenty years or so and was then released.

That's where I came in.

I didn't have a gun, so I improvised. I used a soldering iron to burn him up a little bit, and when I got bored, I strangled him. That was my favorite method of killing because it took a long time and the victim suffered immensely.

It gave them enough time to think about all the mistakes in their lives. It gave them time to regret everything that inevitably led to that fateful moment when I snuff out their lives.

Then there was, of course, the fear of death. That fear that I saw in their eyes was what turned me on the most. I ended up strangling them in front of mirrors, not so much because I wanted them to see their own facial expression but because *I* wanted to see it.

I loved my job.

In a world where being a vigilante would be legal, I could snap a picture of my victim or a selfie with the body in the backdrop and post it on Instagram with the caption *another day at work* or *love my job*, and people would comment things like *slay, queen* and *I'm a huge fan of yours*.

The results of the two victims were nothing like I'd expected them to be.

After the first victim was killed, there was no budge in public support. The media framed it as a murder of a person, not a murder of a criminal. The second victim produced the same results.

I'd had enough by then, and I knew that mindlessly killing criminals would do nothing save put me at risk of getting caught. No, I would need to change my methods because the public was clearly determined to demonize me.

I spent the next few weeks tirelessly looking for my next victim. The list was abundant, but I knew I couldn't choose just anyone. It had to be a big target. It had to be someone that the public considered really, really evil without a sliver of good in them so that, when they fell, everyone rejoices.

But who could be such a target? And how would I be able to bring down someone like that without being caught? Wherever I walked, cops roamed the streets. At night, more so. Even the once-empty streets were now protected by patrolling police vehicles. You couldn't so much as do public urination without getting caught.

My only comfort was that the copycat killer would have a hard time committing any murders in the meantime, too. The longer I waited, however, the greater the chances that they'd kill again and present it as a killing by the Portland Executioner. I was determined to beat them to my next victim, though.

One question that raced through my mind was: Why did they do it? The answers varied, but all of them made sense. They wanted to claim the glory after the path had already been paved. They wanted to put an end to the Executioner.

They wanted to throw the police off by making them believe it was the Executioner and continue killing.

After searching for a while, I realized that the next possible victim had been in front of me the entire time and I had been too blind to see it. Ever since the murder of the pregnant woman, Homicide Detective George Anderson had been popping up in the news almost daily.

It was hard not to notice all the controversy surrounding him. Ever since he was accused of tampering with evidence, taking bribes, and shooting an unarmed suspect, the "defund the police" crowd has been on his ass.

As the lead detective assigned to the Portland Executioner case, he spewed nonsense in the media about having his best team members working on the case, that they were really close to catching the criminal, how they were going to save the country, blah-blah-blah.

Very ironic of him to talk about saving anyone or anything when he had blood on his hands. How in the hell someone like him managed to not just become a detective, but also remain in his position after so many accusations, was beyond me.

He was going to be my next target.

It was very risky—I knew that much—going against a homicide detective, but I knew that it was the only way to prove to the public that the Portland Executioner was good. Step one: Find a target everybody hates. Step two: Kill target. Step three: Watch as the public changes their opinion in support of the Executioner.

Detective Anderson's address was well-known online (Thank God for doxing). He lived in a suburban neighborhood in Beaverton with his wife and son. Even though I didn't know when he went to and from work, I used the information in the media to learn about his whereabouts and routes.

I used that knowledge to visit his home address in Beaverton and stroll around the block while checking how safe the neighborhood was. Anderson usually returned home between 9 p.m. and 11 p.m.

Perks of being a detective in a city so full of crime.

I knew that killing him in his home would be impossible. His house was equipped with alarm systems. This would have to be a quick hitman job on the street. The chances of me being seen by someone were pretty high in the block, so I would need to mask myself fully.

I went out to prepare for the job. I bought an entirely new set of clothes: a pair of cargo pants, noise-canceling boots, a padded jacket, new gloves, a balaclava. I bought these things in separate stores, of course, and paid in cash because, if worse came to worst, the police would then have a harder time tracking me down.

As for the choice of weapon, I contemplated getting a gun, but there was no way I knew how and where to get one. I didn't have a permit, and finding a guy to illegally sell one to me would be as difficult for me as doing pull-ups.

Hell, I wouldn't even know where to start looking. Not like I could walk the streets and ask suspicious-looking people if they knew where I could buy illegal guns (Which was something my ex-coworker did when he wanted to shoot his ex and her lover. Spoiler alert, he got fired and convicted for attempted murder.)

I honestly don't know how people who smoke weed find their contacts. How do you even know who you can talk to about it without the risk of them ratting you out?

A gun was too loud anyway, and in a neighborhood as quiet as Anderson's, it was sure to grab lots of attention. Instead, I decided to take the regular route—the good ol' reliable taser and knife. I was nimble, so I didn't worry about being able to sneak up on George Anderson before he could draw his gun on me.

Doing the preparations for my next kill made me feel like myself again. Even though I hadn't been active for a few weeks (ever since the gang member), it felt as though I'd never stopped. I was overcome by a feeling of excitement like going out on a first date.

Summer had been spending more and more time outside the apartment with Malik, so she hadn't noticed how enthralled I was in preparing (not that she would, anyway).

When the night finally came, I drove to Beaverton and left my car in a secluded parking lot. From there, I walked to the detective's block. It was quiet. No one was outside. I rolled the balaclava over my head and felt its fabric shielding my face from the biting cold.

I ducked behind a nearby tree nestled between two houses close to his home. Let me tell you one thing. I freaking hate the cold. I can tolerate it during winter when I'm taking fast walks between stations and jostling through people, or even jogging in the park, but when I sit in one spot, I start freezing very fast, and I despise it.

That's what happened to me while I waited for the detective. The first thing I felt was the cold air swaddling my eyes exposed by the balaclava. Then, my skin prickled. Pretty soon, the tips of my fingers went numb even though I had gloves on. It wasn't long until the cold settled deep in my body.

I was tempted to stand up and walk a few laps just to warm up, but it was too risky. I'd already heard voices from the adjacent streets and didn't want heads turning in my direction. Any normal citizen would report seeing a person dressed like me to the police.

I kept glancing at the watch, cursing George Anderson for working overtime. It was a little after 10 p.m. when I heard the distant sound of a car's engine. This got my hopes up, and I stood up, my hand patting the pocket where the taser was.

Feel Free To Scream

A car drove by without stopping. It wasn't the detective.

Over the next twenty minutes, two more cars drove by, both times getting my hopes up and then crushing them. But then I saw Detective Anderson's white car (I call it a white car because I had no idea what kind a of car it was.) pulling up to his driveway.

I got up, taser in one hand, knife in the other, patiently waiting as the detective killed the engine. I couldn't risk coming at him yet because he'd see movement in the rearview mirror.

I waited for him to step out of the car.

The detective looked like pretty much any retired detective you'd see in a crime murder documentary: trimmed mustache, flabby face, round belly, and of course, the trademark red tie over the white shirt that all detectives, for some reason, seem to wear.

My window of opportunity was small. I knew I had only a few seconds until he reached the door of his house. I stepped from the cover of the tree, and it was at that moment that I knew there was no turning back.

If the detective saw me, he would most likely insist on seeing my face and questioning me. I'd be taken to the police station, and if I wasn't convicted of being the Portland Executioner, I'd be convicted of attempted murder.

Who, me? Oh, just... taking a nightly stroll. What, the taser? That's just to, uh... defend myself. Lots of stray dogs in the area.

I didn't need to bother being too prudent with my steps because the boots I had bought completely eliminated the noise of my footsteps. Even as I approached the detective, who stood by his car and checked something on his phone, I couldn't help but admire the footwear that helped me be so stealthy.

I was just fifty feet away from him and closing distance fast. Forty feet.

The detective put his phone in his pocket, and then he did something that made me stop dead in my tracks.

He turned around.

Comical confusion washed over his face as our eyes locked in a staring contest. It was one of those moments where I had a split-second thought that if I didn't move he wouldn't notice me. A stupid thought, but I was caught by surprise and didn't know what to do.

I'm the kind of person who likes sticking to the plan. If that plan doesn't work, I usually have a backup plan just in case. But if all my plans from A to Z fail, then I freeze. In all the extensive preparation for the detective's murder, I failed to consider something as simple as him turning around to face me.

Maybe I had gotten rusty or too relaxed.

The next thing I knew, Detective Anderson's hand was reaching for something under his jacket, and then I was staring at the barrel of a gun.

"On the ground! Now!" Anderson shouted with a stern voice.

I could imagine teenage delinquents plopping to the ground at the sound of his quaking voice. I was still frozen. I knew that if I got on the ground, it would all be over. The days of the Portland Executioner would be finished. At least the real Executioner, which would give the copycat killer the freedom to continue twisting my vision.

Something clicked inside me. I spun on my heel and ran toward the cover that I'd been using for the past hour. The detective's voice behind me boomed, ordering me to stop, and then a loud bang echoed in the air.

Something whistled past me, and I vaguely registered that the fucker was shooting. Maybe a warning shot?

My answer came a moment later when I heard another three bangs, these too close to me to be considered warning shots. The son of a bitch was trying to kill me even though I didn't do anything wrong!

I mean, I was going to kill him, sure, but that's not the point. The point is, you can't go trigger-happy because you see a masked figure approaching you from behind at night when you're standing alone in your driveway.

I didn't stop when I was out of the detective's line of sight. I didn't stop as I turned into the adjacent street. In fact, I sprinted until I was five blocks away and I could no longer hear gunshots. I had jumped a few fences and zig-zagged between the houses to skirt the detective.

Only when my lungs and legs could no longer take the physical exertion did I stop in an alley behind a trash container.

I figured there was no way he could run after me that fast and that far—not with that belly in the way. What I was sure of, though, was that he would call for backup. I had to get back to my car, change my clothes, and get the hell out of there.

I was so pissed. I was angry at Anderson and at myself for letting my plan fail like that. That was it. I wouldn't get another chance to kill him, and he would most likely come looking for the masked figure with a vengeance.

I took a step to leave the alley and felt a searing pain jolting through my left calf. My eyes gravitated down, and I noticed that my leg was bleeding. *Shit.* I got woozy. *Don't pass out. Not now.*

On a whim, I dabbed the injury with a glove and raised it to my face, staring in awe at the fingertips that glistened with fresh blood. I guess the detective's bullet hit its mark after all.

I wasn't bleeding badly, but the pain was unbearable. My two biggest concerns were whether I left a trail of blood for the cops to find and how I would reach my car. I took off one glove, made a clump out of it, and stuffed it in my pants to press against the bullet wound.

It hurt like a bitch, but I avoided screaming.

If the cops saw me now, I'd have to surrender. No way I'd be able to run with this leg. Cautiously, I peeked out of the alley toward the street. I heard sirens in the distance. No one else seemed to be outside, so I crossed the street and made my way toward the parking lot.

Either I got really lucky, or the cops didn't think to comb that area because I didn't run into a single person on the street. Never have I been so happy to see the crappy Dodge.

The first thing I did was strip out of all my clothes. I was sticky with sweat, and the cold felt like knives dancing on my skin. My calf was a hot, burning mess. The bullet hole was tiny, but the blood just wouldn't stop trickling. Even small contractions of the muscle caused my leg to spasm in excruciating pain.

Luckily, I always come prepared in case something goes wrong. I pulled out the first aid kit from the trunk and got on the backseat of the Dodge. Its leather seats were so damn cold to the touch. At least, my skin didn't get stuck to them because it was slick with sweat.

I couldn't go to the hospital to get the bullet out; I knew that much. I would be serving myself to them on a platter. I had to get the bullet out myself.

A pair of pliers sat next to me. I had used those to pull out all the teeth from the mouth of a guy who punched his girlfriend so hard she choked on her own teeth. Even bringing the pliers' pointy ends close to my calf made me wince. I could envision them coming to life and talking to me, the blades moving up and down as its lips.

Go on, bitch. What are you waiting for? I can't wait to dig through your muscles in search of a piece of lead. Oh, if I accidentally snip an artery, sorry about that.

Without thinking, I buried the tips of the pliers into my wound. My calf spastically jerked, and I folded my leg in a way that I sat on it so that it couldn't move. The pain blurred my vision. I could feel every nerve in my leg screaming in pain as the metallic tool dug through my flesh.

I felt the jaws coming in contact with something tiny and hard. I tried to grip it, but the small object slipped multiple times. Fresh blood oozed out of my leg abundantly. I knew I couldn't stop. If I pulled out the pliers now, I would have to go through the same pain of entering and digging through it again.

The bullet slithered out of my grip over and over. It, too, came to life and laughed at me.

Aw, you were so close. Try it again. Oh, whoops, guess I slipped out. Too bad.

But then the jaws finally gripped the little bastard firmly. I resisted the urge to yank it out. I didn't want to lose my grip on it. I was also afraid that I might have pinched a blood vessel or something there, and the thought of pulling spaghetti-like strings out of my calf terrified me.

Slowly, I pulled the pliers out as if it was a piece of thread that could snap at any moment.

Just like that, the tool was out of my calf, the jaws covered in blood, and in their bite, a tiny bullet.

This little thing caused so much damage?

I wanted to throw the bullet as far as I could, but the last thing I needed was for someone to find it. I put the pliers and the bullet aside and focused on sterilizing and wrapping up my injury. I thought the worst part was over until I put alcohol on the wound. I had to clamp a hand over my mouth to stop myself from screaming.

Once the wound was bandaged, I decided that I needed a few minutes to take a break even if the whole police department was looking for me.

I fell sideways on the Dodge's backseat and closed my eyes.

Feel Free To Scream

12

THE LETTER

I think I must have passed out for a little bit from the pain and the exhaustion. When I opened my eyes, everything was still the same. The sweat covering my body had dried, and upon getting up, I was met with resistance from the leather seats.

It reminded me of the time I passed out during P.E. at school. One moment, I was playing volleyball, feeling lightheaded as heck; in the next, I opened my eyes to find myself on the ground and the teacher and classmates standing over me, asking if I was okay.

I unstuck myself with a loud squelching sound (Having sex in this car would be so uncomfortable, I figured, for the first time in my life) and got dressed in my "civilian" clothes. The throbbing in my calf persisted, but it was duller than before. I took a look at my bandaged leg and then wiggled my foot up and down to get the calf moving.

Pain stung my leg but less so than before while the bullet was still lodged inside. I tucked all the clothes and items that could incriminate me under the seat. I then sprayed Lysol over the backseats and wiped them until the entire car smelled of citrus.

There; all traces of blood gone. If everything I've seen on CSI was correct, then they'd still be able to locate invisible traces of blood in my car, using ultraviolet light, but it was my blood, so it was okay.

We need to search your car, ma'am.

Search away. Oh, but I gotta warn you I cut myself on a tuna can, so you may find some blood. I know, I shouldn't eat tuna in my car, but it's my guilty pleasure.

With all that done, I got behind the wheel.

Feel Free To Scream

Even though I felt a little woozy, I was good enough to drive. Luckily, I had an automatic car just like ninety-five percent of my fellow countrymen, so my injured foot could take a break.

Hell, I couldn't even imagine using it to constantly squeeze the clutch whenever I needed to shift gears, brake, step on the gas pedal, etc.

I don't even know why car designers make that an option. It's just more work, and more often than not, people don't know how to use the manual gear shifters and end up wasting more gas and doing damage to the car. I mean, that's at least what car experts told me. Not that I would know.

I guess it's for car enthusiasts, no idea.

The first thing I did was stop at the nearest trash container and get rid of the clothes and the bullet. I made sure to bury them deep under the heap of trash, which meant digging in the cold through wet, smelly, sticky things that could have been anything—eggshells, cartons of milk, used condoms...

I like to think it wasn't the last one.

By the time I was done burying the clothes, I looked around for about the hundredth time, went back into my car, rubbed my hands to bring the warmth back to my numb fingers, and drove off.

I spent a little bit of time scrutinizing the car's interior once more just to make sure everything was as clean as I thought it was. It was. I don't half-ass things.

Except when it comes to killing a detective, I distinctly heard the pliers mocking me.

"That was..." I found myself making an excuse to an inanimate object, but I couldn't conjure a proper explanation even to it.

The pliers were still on the seat, their beaks clean. I wanted to chuck them across the parking lot, but they were the only pliers I had, and no matter how rude they were, they saved my life.

I limped into the building and used the elevator for the first time in many months to go back inside the apartment.

Upon entering, I heard hushed voices and giggling in the living room. Summer and Malik turned their heads toward me. I felt like an animal on display in the zoo, but instead of snapping at them, I grinned.

"Hey, sis. You okay? You look a little pale," Summer said.

I remember thinking how, of all the times, she chose the worst one not to be Little Red Riding Hood.

"Uh-huh. Just in a little pain," I said. "Think I pulled a muscle in my calf."

Saying that felt like letting a heavy rock drop out of my hands. I could allow myself to limp without arousing any suspicion. My calf was already in a whole lot of pain just from standing for so long. I hoped blood didn't leak through the bandage because then Summer would see it and then—

Well, who am I kidding? I could still trick her then into believing it wasn't a bullet hole even if she insisted on examining the wound, which I wouldn't let her do.

"Oh, no," Summer said. "Do you need us to take you to the doctor or something?"

"No, no. Everything is fine. You kids enjoy. I'm gonna take a shower and hit the hay."

"Oh, sis?" Summer called out.

I was already halfway to the bathroom and facing away from Malik and Summer. Even spinning around took a lot of effort. I really needed to lie down for a moment and rest my leg. It was probably placebo, though.

It's like when you're jogging. If you know you need to run two miles, your body is going to start screaming only when you're somewhat close to the two-mile mark. But if someone tells you to run four miles, your body will not start complaining until it's close to the goal yet again.

It's like the brain knows what distance the body needs to cross and then stretches the pain so that it becomes unbearable only toward the end. That's what happened to me the night I tried to kill Detective Anderson.

Although the pain in my leg was excruciating the entire time, it only became unbearable as I got closer to the apartment. So when Summer called out to me and I spun around to face her, I smiled even though my teeth were pressed so tightly together that I felt like I would grind them into dust.

"What's up?" I asked, uttering the sentence as fast as I could like skimming the pages of a book to finish reading it sooner.

"You shouldn't go out alone at this time of the night anymore," Summer said.

"It's true. It's dangerous with the Portland Executioner and all," Malik said. "I thought she was good, but she's probably just another attention-seeker."

I bit the inside of my cheek in order to avoid disagreeing with Malik. I wished him and Summer a good night and went to take a shower.

I wanted to take a long bath, but between the failed kill and the pain in my leg, I didn't want to spend too much time soaking. I just wanted to sleep. After showering, I replaced the bandage and went to bed. Even though thoughts swirled through my mind like a tornado through a farm, I fell asleep almost immediately.

Rays of incessant sunlight that peered through my window woke me up. My first thought was, why didn't the alarm ring? I checked my phone through the blurry vision and realized that I hadn't set it in the first place.

It was a little after 9 a.m. and I had to hurry to work. Coffee, as much as I would have loved to have it, would need to wait until I was at the office.

I suppressed a scream when my feet touched the ground. My calf protested in pain, reminding me that it was hurt and that I needed to be careful. I gently put weight on my left foot and took a few steps around the bedroom. I couldn't extend my leg entirely for a full step, but I could walk, so it was okay.

When I stepped into the living room-kitchen area, Summer was already awake. The first thing that I became aware of, and it immediately made my entire body relax, was the smell of coffee.

"Hey, sis. You slept in, so I made you coffee," she said just as the buzzing at the door resounded.

"Who's that?" I asked as I dragged my crippled ass to the counter and cupped the coffee mug with both hands, warming my palms with the steamy liquid.

"Malik. He and I are going dog-walking together." Summer sauntered to the door.

"Wow. You two are inseparable," I said as I took the first sip.

I let the liquid slosh in my mouth for a little bit before swallowing. The door opened, and Malik stood in front in his awkward, tense-shouldered pose, smiling. He wore a thick jacket that made him look like a penguin, and a bear-shaped cap with fully equipped ears and all.

Summer wrapped her arms around him, and they spent a moment smooching. I averted my gaze and focused on the coffee.

"It's cold out, so make sure you get dressed well. Good morning, ma'am," Malik said as he stepped inside and saw me.

He still called me ma'am, which I found adorable.

"Huh, what's this?" Summer was about to close the door when her eyes fell on something on the ground.

She bent down to pick it up, got inside, and closed the door while focusing on the object in her hand.

"It's for you, sis," she said as she handed me an envelope with my name written on it. "I'll be ready in a minute, Malik. Just gotta find my gloves."

"I'd give you my gloves even if it meant getting frostbite on my fingers," Malik said.

"Aww," Summer exclaimed.

Cringe. Cute, but cringe, I thought to myself. I opened the envelope with a shake of my head and pulled out the folded piece of paper. One sentence was written on it, all in capital letters.

STOP KILLING OR SOMEONE YOU LOVE WILL BE NEXT.

I darted my eyes across the message multiple times then checked the backside, which was blank. Then I read the single sentence again. It was, once again, one of those moments where I waited for the context to change the more I read it, but it remained the same, no matter what.

Summer and Malik's voices filled the backdrop of the room while my mind slowly reached a panicked crescendo.

"Summer?" I called out with a voice that sounded petulant and scared. Summer and Malik turned to face me. "Where did you get this?" I raised the letter.

"It was on the ground in front of the door." Summer shrugged.

"Not in the mailbox?" I asked even though I already knew the answer.

I mean, I'd seen her bend down and pick up the letter, but my mind refused to believe that it was at the front door and that it was meant for me.

"Nope, right in front of the door," Summer confirmed.

I stared at the letter for a moment, the words no longer bearing any meaning. I looked up at Malik and asked, "Malik, did you see anyone else in the building?"

"Well, there was an old lady on the first floor, and—"

"No, I mean someone coming up to our apartment. Someone who maybe looked like they were lost or anything like that?"

It took a lot of effort to sound calm. I didn't want my questions to sound accusatory, and I also didn't want to convey urgency about the letter, so I played it cool.

"No one like that, ma'am."

"Did anyone perhaps enter the building with you?"

"Nope."

"Do you think it's possible someone walked by you but you don't remember?"

Malik shook his head. I could see that he was starting to become uncomfortable, so I smiled and stopped questioning him.

"Sis? Are you okay? What was in the envelope?" Summer asked.

I looked up and flashed her a courteous grin. "Oh, just some bills. But they're early, and I'm baffled about how they ended up at the door is all."

"Come to think of it, someone rang the doorbell just a couple of minutes ago before Malik, but when I opened it, no one was there," Summer said.

I nodded.

Now, I have to explain a little bit about our building for you to understand why I was so upset about the letter. Yes, the contents of the letter upset me, but how the letter reached our apartment also upset me.

First of all, in order to get inside the parking lot, you need to have either an electronic key or know the passcode. Once you're in, you need to have another key and another passcode to actually enter the building.

That means that someone managed to bypass two points of security and sneak inside just to deliver a letter to me. And that *someone* was the copycat killer, no doubt about it.

He knew where I lived.

I felt sick to my stomach. I didn't even get the chance to take a second sip of my coffee before excusing myself and leaving the apartment. Mrs. Kurtz was in front of her apartment. She was often in front of the door, so I asked her if she'd seen anyone suspicious.

She said something about flyer-delivery guys coming in and out and started rambling about the building always being loud and how the police need to be informed of the racket, etc.

I interrupted her mid-sentence to thank her and was then on my way. Okay, so the guys who deliver commercial items to the mailboxes (or someone pretending as such) were the biggest culprits. Usually, what those guys do is ring randomly on the intercom and ask if they can go inside to put the papers in the promotional mailbox. It was possible that the copycat killer presented himself as the flyer guy and one of the tenants let him inside.

On my way out, I glanced at the security office where a guard who looked like he was old enough to have witnessed the Declaration of Independence sat, reading a newspaper.

After work, I could talk to him about letting me see the camera footage. There were too many suspects like this, but if it was one of the flyer people who delivered that letter, then I would know because they never went past the promotional mailbox, which was at the entrance.

I barely registered the pain in my leg as I drove to work. *STOP KILLING OR SOMEONE YOU LOVE WILL BE NEXT.* I swear to God, if they so much as looked at Summer, I would have cut off their balls and stuffed them in their mouth.

My mind was so focused on the letter sitting on the passenger's seat that I nearly caused a traffic accident. To be fair, he was kind of a dick for hitting the brakes so suddenly, but still.

STOP KILLING OR SOMEONE YOU LOVE WILL BE NEXT.

When I arrived at my destination, I placed the letter in the glove compartment. As much as I wanted to destroy it, I was determined to study it, perhaps compare the handwriting online so I could at least tell what gender the killer was.

Work was pretty much the same. I flashed my trademark PR grins, I had meetings, and then just before lunch, Cindy knocked on my office door to tell me someone was here to see me.

I immediately recognized the trimmed mustache, the flabby cheeks, the incongruously large belly, and of course, the red tie.

"Good day, ma'am. I'm Detective George Anderson," he said.

Feel Free To Scream

13

INTERROGATION

It was a good thing I was sitting because I felt like I might collapse. I tried to hide the shock on my face in front of the detective because I knew he would read everything about me just as I would read everything about him.

"What do you want?" I asked, deciding not to give him my fake grin because I knew he would probably be able to see through it.

"I'm here to ask you a few questions. Is it okay if I sit down?" he asked, pointing to the chair.

It sounded polite enough, but I knew he would do it regardless of my response. I gave him a subtle nod of approval, and he took a seat in the chair in front of my desk. That chair was reserved for people with whom I had one-on-ones, mostly interviewees or coworkers who I needed to give a performance evaluation.

Now, it felt as though the tables had turned (no pun intended) and I was on the interrogated side.

For the first time, I was able to see Anderson's face in detail. It was riddled with crags and marks of old age, even though he couldn't have been more than forty. Those were marks of someone who had seen the monstrosity of mankind day after day.

At the same time, there was something stern, not-gonna-take-your-bullshit on his face that made me feel weak like last night when he pointed his gun at me. As he stared at me, I couldn't help but feel like we were old acquaintances who hadn't spoken in years.

The indifferent look he gave me was hard to read, but I knew one thing for sure: He was here to question me, not arrest me. If he knew I was the one who attacked him, he would have walked in, flashed his badge, and said something along the lines of, "You're under arrest for *insert crimes in blank lines.*"

That gave me a sense of control, as wobbly as it was. I leaned back in my chair, assuming the most relaxed body language I could, and said, "What can I do for you?"

"I'm here about the recent murders that took place. You probably heard of the Portland Executioner. I'm the lead detective assigned to the case."

"Yes, I know all about you. Kind of hard to avoid seeing you on all the major channels, given your history and affinity toward cameras."

Anderson's mouth slightly contorted into a smirk. He mimicked my movement and leaned back in his chair. It creaked and I wondered if it would break under his weight. That would have been hilarious; for a detective to collapse onto his back and then wiggle like a beetle while I calmly walked out of the office.

"Can you tell me where you were last night?" he asked.

I refused to look away under his gaze. That would only show that I was uncomfortable, and I wasn't about to do that.

"I went out for a jog," I said.

"Where?"

"Willamette."

The detective continued leering at me. I knew what he was trying to do. It's the oldest trick in the book. Stare at someone with a blank face and make them uncomfortable; pretty soon, they'll add more information just to fill the awkward silence and potentially expose themselves. I used that trick all the time with candidates who weren't talkative.

"You always go jogging that late?" Anderson asked.

"Most of the time. I'm kind of busy, Detective. Would you mind cutting to the chase?"

In my mind, I prayed *Don't ask to see my leg... don't ask to see my leg* while I sternly stared at him.

Anderson scratched his nose and then brought his hand down. My eyes fell on the badge clipped to his belt that painfully dug into the underside of his belly. I wondered how he was not bothered by it. Maybe he was and he just didn't want to show it in front of me.

"Last night, someone came to my home and tried to kill me," he said.

"Not a surprise. You made a lot of enemies," I said.

"It was a woman. She managed to run away, but I have reason to believe it was the Portland Executioner and not some unrelated murder attempt."

I blinked.

"Here's what I managed to compile so far," the detective said as he leaned forward. "The Portland Executioner is a woman, someone who probably works hours similar to yours."

"I don't see how that has anything to do with me."

"Oh, but I think it does. You see, the first victim was someone known to you. Someone who sexually assaulted your sister, correct?"

I nodded.

"The court didn't bring any results in sentencing the offender. I can see how that would make someone angry. I can see how someone might try to take justice into their own hands because the law failed to do so. Do you think that's a possibility?"

"It may be. A lot of people hated Robert."

"We found similar patterns in subsequent murders, like in the case of James Carter."

I remained silent.

"There was also the murder of the pedophile, Jeff Lee. Have you heard about him?" he asked.

"I have. Not horrible news if you ask me."

The detective ogled me for a moment as if thinking about what to say next.

"Where were you the night he was killed?"

"Detective Anderson, that was a long time ago." I snorted. "I don't remember what I had for lunch yesterday, let alone where I was the night some criminal was murdered."

The detective nodded. If he was exasperated with the interrogation leading nowhere, then he did a pretty good job of hiding it.

"You had a business trip to San Francisco recently, correct?"

"Yes."

I didn't like where this was going.

"What was the purpose of the trip?" Anderson asked.

"Making a presentation for our business partners."

"I see. How long did you stay there?"

"A week."

He already knew all of this, of course. He was just trying to catch me in a smaller lie so that he could then pressure me into confessing something bigger.

"You stayed there for a week," he said. "Andrej Milic was murdered that week. No witnesses, no tangible forensic evidence. You knew Andrej, correct?"

"I don't think so," I said.

"Really? Are you sure?" Anderson frowned.

"Yes, I'm sure," I repeated, impatient more than I was scared.

"We have witnesses who saw you interacting with him in Arabian Nights the night he was killed."

"They saw the wrong person. I never go out there."

"What if I told you we have video evidence of your Dodge parked nearby?"

I knew for a fact that was a lie because I deliberately walked to Arabian Nights exactly because of cameras. Anderson was trying to get me to confess on a bluff.

"Like I said, wrong person."

"And you've never met Andrej Milic before?"

"I've heard of him on the news. If you're suggesting something, Detective, then say it openly."

Anderson leaned back and cleared his throat. I realized that I was tapping my uninjured foot on the ground nervously. I stopped myself from doing it.

"I'm not suggesting anything yet, ma'am. I'm just asking you if you know anything about these murders that might help us resolve the case."

In detective words, that actually means confess so we can call it a day and go home earlier.

"I'm afraid I can't help you, Mr. Anderson," I calmly said.

"All right. Is there anything you want to tell me? Something that might help with the investigation?"

Yeah. I received the copycat killer's letter this morning.

"No. Nothing," I said.

"Okay. Just one more thing. The recent murder of the pregnant woman... We know for a fact it's not the same killer."

"It's not?" I pretended to be surprised.

"No."

"Then why aren't you telling the public about it?"

"We want the killer to think he has the upper hand, get reckless, and then we'll catch him."

The detective was lying because then why would he tell me, a potential suspect, crucial information like that. The reason was that he wanted to lull me into a false sense of security by shifting blame elsewhere.

"In fact, we don't even know if the copycat homicide was done by a man or a woman, but we're looking into it. Let me tell you one thing. The Portland Executioner... the *real* Portland Executioner has done a good thing here. She cleaned the streets for us and made the town a safer place.

The crime rate in Portland has dropped by twenty-eight percent, which is a huge improvement. Don't you agree?"

"I don't like to get philosophical."

"I see. Well, either way, the Portland Executioner, unlike the copycat killer, killed only bad people. But that still makes her a murderer. They both need to be caught and tried for their crimes."

"You have such a strong resolution to catch those criminals, Detective. Was that the same kind of resolution you had when you tampered with the evidence to get Shaun Floyd convicted? And if so, what's stopping you from doing it again?"

I saw the detective's face slightly changing before going back to its reticent self. He then smiled, stood up, and said, "That'll be all, ma'am. If we have any more questions, we'll contact you."

He nodded and waded toward the door. Just as he reached the threshold, he stopped and turned around.

"Oh, and one more thing, ma'am. We received an anonymous tip from the killer that he's going to kill someone tonight. I suggest you don't stay out too late," he said and, without further elaborating, walked out of the office.

I wanted to breathe the deepest sigh of relief that I could, but I didn't know if I was being watched. I lowered my head to the papers and continued signing them while replaying the conversation with the detective in my head.

He had me on the list of suspects. Hell, maybe even knew I was the one who did it, and he just didn't have enough evidence to arrest me. He would keep an eye on me, I knew that much. That meant my hands were tied, and I wouldn't be able to kill anymore – at least, not for a while.

It felt like the walls were closing in on me. The detective on one side, the copycat killer on the other. *STOP KILLING OR SOMEONE YOU LOVE WILL BE NEXT. We received an anonymous tip from the killer.* The most alluring solution, at that moment, was to just stop being the Portland Executioner.

I tried helping the public, and they spat in my face. Now, my sister or someone else close to me might be in danger because of my actions. The letter said to stop killing. That seemed simple enough. And with the detective pressing down on me, not killing seemed like the easiest thing in the world.

Except it wasn't.

I almost convinced myself that my days as the Portland Executioner had come to an end, that I had barely dodged multiple bullets (both figuratively and literally), and that I should continue living my life as the director of recruiting and find a guy to marry and have kids with.

Aunt Mary would be so proud to hear my thoughts.

No. That's not what I wanted. Returning to the boring life where I'd work a corporate job, cook lunch, and pay taxes was not for me. Yes, I excelled at work, but I was not destined for it.

Shame draped me at the realization that I was so close to giving in to the temptation. I was the Portland Executioner, and if the police didn't plan on proving that the copycat killer and I were not the same, then I would. I would save that victim tonight, whoever it was.

Even if it meant getting caught.

Feel Free To Scream

14

CULPRIT

Despite the ton of work piled on me, I couldn't get anything done. Between the pain in my calf and the worry that overwhelmed me, focusing on work turned out to be impossible.

So instead, I did some research on Detective George Anderson and the public backlash that he suffered. Everything I already knew sat online, but there was one piece of information that I overlooked somehow.

The pregnant woman who had been killed by the copycat killer, Danielle Metzger, was actually one of the leading figures of the group that so openly criticized Anderson and wanted to defund the police. She had been very active with the protests where she was on the front lines with a megaphone in her hand and had also done multiple interviews.

Needless to say, she was a thorn in Anderson's side, and her death worked greatly to his advantage. In fact, with her gone, the group grew silent, scattered, and leaderless. That's not to say the group had no other leaders. They just stopped making appearances after Dannielle Metzger's death.

Their promises to "tear down the entire police department and rebuild it from scratch if the government didn't comply" went down the drain at the first sign of trouble. Economy students, am I right? They read one book by Karl Marx, and all of a sudden they think they know everything that's wrong with our country and how to fix it.

Anyway, another interesting piece of news popped up as I scrolled.

On top of the already known accusations, there was one that Anderson and his buddies at the force swept under the rug. The rumor said that a suspected drug dealer had evidence planted at his house by the detective, after which he was shot to death. The detective explained that the suspect had been armed, and no one second-guessed it.

The article exhaustively explained why the planted evidence couldn't possibly have been the dealer's and that he was never armed. Also, the article said the dealer never was a dealer in the first place. The reason why the detective killed him? The dealer threatened to expose his crimes to the public if he didn't pay him a certain sum.

It sounded far-fetched at first, but the more I read it, the more it sounded believable. The article, whomever it was written by, covered every possible plot hole. If this was how all conspiracy theories worked, I could understand how someone might become an anti-vaxxer or a flat-earther.

Maybe I was just desperate, but I wanted to believe that the detective was, in fact, the copycat killer. Maybe not him personally, but someone he might send to assassinate Danielle Metzger.

It would make sense for him to use the opportunity during the Portland Executioner's spree to kill his own political enemy and blame it on the killer without arousing any suspicion.

After all, he said they didn't tell the public about the copycat because they wanted to surprise the killer, but now I believed the reason for the secrecy was something else. Perhaps the detective convinced everyone on the investigation team that there never was a copycat killer and, instead, blamed Danielle's death on the Portland Executioner.

So then, why did he tell me about the copycat? Simple. To see my reaction.

If he was indeed the one responsible for the death of the pregnant woman, then I would be up against a formidable foe. Eliminating the detective would no longer be as simple as I thought because I blew my chance the previous night.

That still pissed me off but also made me feel like a fool. The pain in my leg was here to remind me of it.

I couldn't wait for work to be over that day. As soon as I was out of the office, I felt like I could finally breathe freely again. I rushed back home, and the first thing I did before returning to the apartment was barge into the security office.

Or at least, I tried, but instead, I almost slammed my face on the opaque glass pane that said "SECURITY."

I noticed the *BE BACK SOON* sign plastered to the door and felt stupid for not noticing it before. No use waiting for the security guard. If the old man went out for a piss break, he would be gone for a long time.

I'd seen him walking and once had the bad luck of waiting for him to get out of the elevator so I could take it. The elevator doors had automatically started closing three times until I stopped them with my foot and waited for the guard to get out.

As soon as I was in front of the apartment, my gaze gravitated toward the *Alohomora* doormat. No warning letters, tripwires, landmines, anything like that. Even before I stepped inside, I heard the muffled voices of Malik and Summer.

They had become a symbiotic entity, thriving on each other. I felt a pang of anger directed at Summer. All of a sudden, she had a boyfriend, and now her life revolved around him. That was a recipe for heartbreak.

Just like with Robert.

The two of them were dressed in winter clothes, visibly ready to go out somewhere.

Feel Free To Scream

"Where're you headed?" I asked as I limped toward the couch.

"We're going to Washington Park," Summer said.

"At this time? During this weather? Summer, you hate the cold. I mean, you're named after the hottest season, for crying out loud."

"I know, but there's a cabin there that Malik reserved for us. We're going to spend the night there."

"It's kinda dangerous out there these days, no?" I asked, trying not to be too direct.

"It is," Summer confirmed. "That poor pregnant woman who got killed. Danielle, right? You know, Malik knew her."

"You did?" I raised an eyebrow.

Malik's cheeks turned ruddy, and I didn't need to ask what that meant.

"Well, we used to be friends, yeah," Malik said after clearing his throat.

"Summer, going out is not a good idea. Why don't you guys stay here instead?"

Summer looked offended. "Malik went through a lot of trouble to get that reservation. What's the big deal? We're just going to spend the night by the fire. Right, Malik?"

"I'll return her in one piece, ma'am," Malik said as he wrapped an arm around Summer.

"Summer..." I started but found no words to argue.

I then remembered this was Summer. She was going to do things her own way, and the more I told her not to do it, the more she would. Malik was with her, and he would keep her safe.

Besides, Summer would be safe tonight. The copycat killer had sent a tip to the cops, which meant he already had a victim in mind. It was my job to save that person.

"Keep your phone on and all times," I said. "And when I call you, I expect you to answer, no matter what time it is. Got it?"

"Okay, Mom." Summer rolled her eyes. She looked like she was simply relieved that I complied with her decision. "Let's go, Marshmallow," she said as she grabbed Malik by the hand and yanked him toward the door.

Cringe, I thought to myself.

As soon as they were out, I ate some leftover lasagna, just enough bites to chase the nagging hunger away, and then raced downstairs to the security room.

The old fossil sitting at the desk looked up at me with the reflexes of a braindead shark. He opened his mouth to say something, but the words weren't coming out. He already had one foot in the grave, and I had no intention of waiting for him to finish his sentence, warning, question, whatever just in time to have the other foot there as well, so I interrupted him.

"I need to see the camera footage," I said and then quickly added before he could protest, "Someone's been lurking near my apartment, and I need to know who it is."

The old security guard looked at the monitors with an expression that someone who lied on their resume to get the job and now had no idea what to do would. He pointed a trembling hand at the computer and said, "Be my guest. I don't know how to use this technology, anyway."

"Thank you," I said in passing and leaned down toward the keyboard and mouse.

At first, I didn't quite understand how to review the old footage. Asking the old man would yield about as useful results as teaching a raccoon to perform a somersault, so I fiddled with it until I found the right options.

From there, it was pretty easy to find the right time and check the security footage. There were four cameras in total—one overlooking the street, one at the parking lot, one at the entrance to the building, and one in the hallway where the mailboxes were.

I could view all four simultaneously, and the image, although somewhat pixelated, was good enough to recognize faces. Not as good as in spy movies when they zoom in and the quality just keeps getting better, but good enough to recognize Anderson if he stopped by to drop that letter.

I remembered what time I woke up and fast-forwarded, carefully checking each person who appeared on the cameras. The security guard interrupted me a few times by asking what I was looking for. Nice of him to try to be helpful, but he was only distracting me.

Not that he would know, anyway. When he wasn't reading the newspaper or Playboy magazines, he was loudly snoring. If anyone wanted to rob the building, they could take every piece of furniture out of the apartment, leaving only the lightbulb, and still not wake him up.

My phone rang. I picked it up without looking at the caller's name.

"Yes?" I asked, impatient.

I was ready to tell the person off if it was someone from work.

"Good evening. We're calling to ask if you'd like to participate in a questionnaire," a feminine voice said. "We're a company working on building a brand for…"

I tuned out after that. I knew that the woman on the other end would breathlessly talk about their products and then, in a not-so-subtle way, ask me to pay for something or whatever. She seemed to go on forever and I really needed both hands.

"Sorry, not interested," I said and hung up before she could get a chance to try to change my mind.

As I reviewed the cameras, I noticed that tenants had left the building, but no one except Malik entered the entire morning. I rewound to check the earlier hours. Some people left the building to go to work at five and six o'clock (poor fuckers), but no one entered.

Come on, Detective Anderson. When did you come to the building?

I closed my eyes and thought for a moment. Could the letter have been at the door last night when I returned and I simply missed it in all the pain? No, that wasn't possible.

I had the distinct habit of always looking down at the *Alohomora* doormat while unlocking the door. Last night was no exception. I remembered because the matt was crooked, and despite the pain in my foot, I set it into a proper position.

I guess it's some form of OCD or something. Kind of like those people who can't step on cracks because they think something bad will happen.

No one had entered the building between last night and this morning. I checked the footage on fast-forward (It took about an hour, and by then, the old man had fallen asleep and was calmly snoring.) and I came to one conclusion that every ounce of my being refused to believe.

I'd been focused on the wrong person this entire time.

The way Malik nervously looked around on the security footage; the way he looked like he hesitated when entering each door; the way he even glanced at one of the cameras...

It was him.

He put the letter in front of the door.

STOP KILLING OR SOMEONE YOU LOVE WILL BE NEXT.

We received an anonymous tip from the killer.

He plans on killing tonight.

Tonight.

Tonight.

He plans on killing tonight.

Feel Free To Scream

The words reverberated in my skull like a fly trapped in a room and ramming the window over and over. It was never Detective Anderson.

I find the Portland Executioner extremely fascinating.

How could I have been so stupid? Malik had already decided who his next victim was.

He and Summer were long-since gone.

15

RUSH

By the time I burst out the front door of the building, it had started to rain. Not heavy rain, mind you, which I preferred, but the annoying drizzle that irritates your face like a sprinkling system and makes the roads slick enough for the traffic to slow down.

I had tried calling Summer twice by the time I had reached the bottom of the stairs. She wasn't answering. She wasn't even out properly, and already she was breaking the only rule I told her to follow.

I jumped in the Dodge, started it, and drove off. I called Summer three more times while speeding down the road. It went straight to voicemail.

"Summer, when you get this message, please call me back immediately. It's an emergency," I said and hung up.

Angry drivers honked at me, and I was pretty sure one of them shouted something about me slithering out of the abortion bucket. The fact that I even heard that part over the cars, the honking, and the rain told me he had rolled down the window just to shout that sultry insult at me.

"Come on, Summer. Come on, dammit!" I said as I intermittently stared at the road and the phone on the passenger's seat.

Every glint of the street lights that the screen reflected caused me to snap toward the phone because I thought it had lit up with someone calling me. By the time I got to Goose Hollow, a loud ringing filled the car. It was the most beautiful sound I had ever heard.

"Hello?!" I answered, my eyes fixed on the road.

"Good evening," a calm, feminine voice not belonging to Summer said. "We're calling to ask if you'd like to participate in a questionna—"

"Oh, fuck off!" I yelled into the phone before hanging up and tossing the phone back on the seat.

I was close to Washington Park now anyway. I drove so recklessly that I ended up bumping the car into another parked vehicle. Sorry, but not really. I'll pay for the damages later.

The moment I stepped out, I felt the heavy pattering of the cold droplets on my head. The drizzle had turned into moderate rain that already had my clothes and hair soaking. I ran through the entrance into the park and followed the trail with as light of a jog as my injured calf would allow me.

I love the outdoors, but only during the daytime.

As beautiful and serene as nature was during the daytime, it was just as creepy and cold during the night. There was something about the naked trees with their skeletal branches clustered all around you and threatening to disorient you. Something about the sounds of the creatures that only came out at night. Something about the fact that natural light gets blocked out so much that only thick darkness remains.

The park had a brightly illuminated trail, yes, but I was still uncomfortable with the darkness that crept all around me.

Looking left and right toward the trees made me feel like there were hundreds and hundreds of predators—black shadowy leopards and wolves—sitting there, watching me, drooling, just waiting for me to step out of the light (or for one of the lights shielding me to give out) so they could tear up their meal and reach the best parts before the others do.

I hadn't realized that my hand was in my purse, fingers closed around the taser. The pepper spray and knife were in there, too, but the taser made me feel the safest. My calf warned me with each step that I was overdoing it and should just call it a day and go back before it was too late.

Come on, kiddo. You don't like the woods anyway. And this rain is really messing me up. It was the taser that spoke in my mind, but then the knife joined in, too, saying something about getting rust all over its beautiful steel.

"Shut up," I said aloud as I walked even faster.

I reached a forked path with a signpost that said the cabins were down the left trail, just half a mile away. Just a little more. I hoped to God that Malik was the kind of murderer who took his sweet time making preparations.

Hell, I was so desperate that I didn't even care if I was too late to stop him from raping Summer, but I absolutely had to get there in time before he killed her. Yes, she would probably be scarred for life and never have another boyfriend ever again, but she would be alive.

Still, the thought of that sicko forcing himself on my little sister after she had already endured one trauma made panic boil at the pit of my stomach. Panic and anger, as black as the forest around me.

Just as I broke into a jog, a sound behind stopped me. I froze and spun. Footsteps echoed somewhere behind me. One, two, three steps, and then they stopped as if sensing that I was aware of them.

Come on, not now. I didn't care if this place was haunted at night or anything like that, but I wanted it to wait until I saved my sister before it started booing me or levitating objects in front of my face.

For a moment, I waited and stared down the trail, expecting something nine feet tall, ungracefully skinny, with a horned head, and with hands reaching all the way to the ground to appear in the light.

You're thinking Wendigo, I thought to myself. Or was it Skinwalker? I didn't care. All I knew was I cursed the day I discovered Unit #522's YouTube channel and listened to his narration of allegedly true stories.

While listening to the stories from the comfort of my bed, tucked under a thick blanket (because monsters can't get there, right?) and with all my doors locked, I felt no fear. In fact, the videos helped me fall asleep.

Now, in the middle of the forest at night, hearing distant footsteps, I was more of a believer. Ironic that the Portland Executioner was afraid of superstitious stuff, right? Well, I'm only human. I'm sure Ted Bundy had his fears, too.

I mean, not that I should be compared to Bundy, but you get the point.

Since the footsteps didn't come again, I turned on my heel and hurried toward the cabins. Almost as soon as I did, the footsteps came again like an annoying mosquito that waits for you to turn off the light so it can suck your blood.

At first, I thought it was the echo of my own shoes, but when they came in irregular intervals, I knew someone was following me. The faster I ran, the faster the footsteps following me became.

I looked behind once, then twice, and then stopped when I caught the outline of a cape slinking out of light's reach and merging with the darkness. My heart leapt into my throat because I recognized the silhouette of the trench coat even without seeing it clearly.

James Carter's ghost was back. It wanted revenge because I killed it.

Now, I have to mention that James Carter never made me feel afraid. I was very uncomfortable around him, yes, but never scared. Even when he brandished his weeaboo sword when we were alone in the alleys the night I killed him, I didn't feel threatened by him.

But now, when I saw him stalking me, coming closer, I genuinely felt so frightened that I could feel my hand in the purse trembling violently.

I remembered a conversation I once had with an ex-coworker of mine who used to be military. We talked about the supernatural and unexplained mysteries, which is not a topic I really like discussing because I find it ridiculous.

You know, I'm a big guy. And I've fought with guys bigger than me and guys who were armed to the teeth. I have no problem with that. But if you tell me this house is haunted, I will be ten miles away before you've finished that sentence, he said.

It gave me a weird sense of solace—knowing that it was okay to be scared of something like that. I wanted to tell James to come out so I could kill him a second time, but I wasn't sure if I'd be able to kill him a second time.

I mean, can you kill something that's already dead? Maybe banish it to the void or something by performing a certain ritual. I wasn't in the mood to play Ed and Lorraine Warren and mess around with a Ouija board every time I killed someone.

Save Summer, you idiot.

Too much time had gone by, and with each stop I made, my sister's chances of surviving were decreasing.

I turned around and broke into a jog. My hand was out of the purse, the taser at the ready. I wouldn't turn around anymore unless the footsteps got really close.

The trail's end was in sight. In front of me, a vast open area expanded with cabins messily clustered and facing in various directions. The lights peered through the windows of one of the cabins. The moment I stepped off the trail and onto the cabin area, I slowed down, already winded.

Funny how we can go jogging miles and miles, but when it's running on terrain we're not used to, we get tired too easily. Also, I have no idea why I thought I'd be safe just because I reached the cabin area.

A part of me must have thought that James Carter's ghost would simply bump into an invisible barrier just before reaching me and, like in the movies, would leave, defeated for the moment, and bide its time until it could catch me again.

That was a stupid theory. But then again, thinking I saw a ghost was just as equally stupid. I didn't have time for that right now. Summer was in need of rescuing.

I turned to the cabin and shambled toward it—the final stop. As I stared at the wooden structure, I thought about how the only thing missing was a bolt of lightning to explode in the sky and a maniacal cackle to fill the air.

Nope, too movie-like, I realized.

My leg was pulsating with annoying pain, but I had no intention of stopping. Not until Summer was safe. I looked back once more to see if James Carter (or any other ghosts) were behind me, following me.

I almost expected to see translucent figures of my victims standing in the rain, casting their judgmental glares in my direction. Did I regret, at that moment, killing those people? Not one bit. They got what they deserved.

Was I scared shitless? Absolutely. But fear for my own safety allayed the moment I pushed the wooden doors open and stumbled into the cabin.

With the taser pointed in front of me—Jesus, my hand trembled like I had Parkinson's disease—I scrutinized the interior. There were no spilled buckets of blood soaking on the wooden floor. No dead bodies splayed and staring vacuously into empty space.

"Summer?!" I called out.

Desperation nestled itself deep in my gut at the thought of the cabin being empty and me being in the wrong place. I went into the other room. There she stood, my little sister, in front of the lit fireplace, her face coated with disbelief and shock.

My eyes gravitated to Malik's lifeless body at her feet.

16

LITTLE RED RIDING HOOD

"What are you doing?" Summer asked, her tone accusatory.

"What am *I* doing? What are *you* doing?!" I countered, gesturing to Malik.

A deep, red line decorated his throat, and gallons of blood spilled on the ground below him. His eyes stared at the ceiling. It was a well-known look to me.

"I fucking knew it," I said as I shook my head. "I knew it was you."

"What are you talking about?" Summer asked as she hid the bloodstained knife in her hand behind her back.

I rolled my eyes. Mostly, I was just relieved that Malik was the victim and Summer the killer and not the other way around. Still, this created other problems that needed to be dealt with.

"Seriously, sis. Why did you come here?" Summer asked.

"Because I thought you were in danger!" I said, outraged. "I thought Malik was going to kill you, and then I raced to get here, and then I realized just a few minutes ago that it was you all along, I mean... fuck me! It was you all along. You sent me that letter, and you're the copycat killer. I was just too fucking blind to see it."

"Little Red Riding Hood, huh?" Summer grinned. "I bet you never thought I could do something like this."

"Nope. You had me, I gotta say."

"But how did you figure out it was me?"

"I reviewed the footage of the cameras. And I know Danielle Metzger was Malik's ex. Did you kill her because she was pregnant with Malik's kid?"

"Well, I mean... that was part of the reason, but—"

"Jesus Christ, Summer," I pinched my nose bridge. "You can't kill people like that. How long do you think it's gonna take until the police figure out you're a potential suspect? And now Malik... You're still Red Riding Hood." I shook my head.

"Well... I—I didn't—" Summer stuttered. "Okay, but both Danielle and Malik were bad people. Why do you think I started dating him in the first place?"

"What?" I frowned.

The fire crackled, and silence ensued for a moment.

"That's right!" Summer finally said with vigor. "He was a registered sex offender. And Danielle had her own offshore company that she used for money laundering. What, you think I'd just kill innocent people like that?"

"Oh, Summer..." I said, suddenly feeling like I was completely out of strength.

She'd made so many amateur mistakes, holy shit. If only she'd come to me and asked for advice, I would have helped her. But this isn't one of those things you can openly talk about to your sibling, right?

Hey sis, I'm thinking of jumping on this Portland Executioner trend. Wanna help me out a little bit? No, no, I can do the killing on my own. I just need to know how to remove the evidence. Okay. Thanks, sis. You're the best.

"You're not too clean, either," Summer said.

"What are you talking about?"

Now it was Summer's turn to roll her eyes. "Come on. You think I didn't see all the shady stuff you bought? All the nights you went out and then the victims appearing in the news the next morning? That affectionate smile that you have on your face whenever you see something online about the Portland Executioner like you're chatting with a guy you like?" She raised a finger to her lips.

"Shut up!" I said, my cheeks burning hot. "The Portland Executioner is doing a good thing!"

"I know. I wanted to follow in your footsteps. You killed Robert, and I was so grateful. I wanted to do something for you, too. I wanted you to be proud of me."

Her voice quivered toward the end, and a glint appeared in her eye.

"Summer..." I started, feeling warm tears filling my own eyes.

I wasn't sad or particularly emotional or anything like that. It's just that whenever I heard someone crying, I automatically cried. I sighed. I felt bad for attacking Summer, but I also felt a warm sensation in my chest. I wanted to hug her tightly.

"I *am* proud of you," I said, my own voice trembling like a leaf in the wind. "I mean, look. You killed Malik all on your own. You're really growing up."

I figured this wasn't a pep talk that one would normally have with a family member. It's usually pride and admiration about the person in question learning to ride a bike, traveling on their own, getting their driver's license, etc.

The "aww, it's her first kill" moment gave me the Addams Family kind of vibe.

Look, it's sunny outside, what a beautiful day!

Close the windows, and stay away from them!

"We're going to need to work on your soft skills, though," I said.

"You mean, soft kills?" Summer flashed a conniving grin.

"Stop."

I wiped a tear from my eye and sniffled. Summer's lip quivered. I wanted to tell her again to stop and that I was only sniffling because I was out in the rain and caught a cold, but she'd see through my lies.

We hugged.

A slam came from the entrance. Heavy footsteps resounded in the cabin, and then—

Detective Anderson stood in front of Summer and me, his gun pointed at us, a look of fury swaddling his flabby face.

"I got you now, Aileen Wuornos!" he said.

His trench coat was wet and muddy.

I snorted. "Please. Don't compare me to that poser."

I knew there was no point in pretending now. I mean, I could, but Detective Anderson was here for a reason. At the back of my mind, I knew it was probably him tailing me, but I was too concerned about Summer to care.

"Hands in the air, or I swear to God I'll unload this entire clip in you," Anderson said.

"Calm down, detective. Let's talk about this for a moment," I said as I raised my hands.

"Shut up!" Anderson commanded.

I didn't like the way his finger rested stiffly on the trigger. It was as if he contemplated shooting and then asking questions. Given his history, that's exactly what I expected him to do, so I was kind of ready for a bullet to the forehead.

Honestly, better than spending fifteen years on death row, only to be executed in an ungraceful way and have low-budget, money-grabbing documentaries made about me. Seriously, those serial killer documentaries are so corny.

The man enters the car with his new date. Little does he know he should have brought better protection. *dramatic music playing*

I knew that getting out of this predicament wouldn't be easy. One hopeful part of me believed that the detective had come here alone and unbeknownst to his coworkers. He had to if he wanted to kill the killer without any witnesses.

That meant that Summer and I could still make it out of this without getting caught. In the worst-case scenario, though, I would take the fall for all the murders and let Summer live her life normally.

The legacy of the Portland Executioner would not end, though. The murders would stop, but my legend would live on.

"Oh, thank God!" I heard Summer's voice next to me.

She skipped past me and stopped next to a confused Anderson.

"Thank goodness you're here!" she said with a voice that sounded so fake I could almost imagine everything around her being theatrical props. "She killed my poor boyfriend! Slit his throat right in front of me! She was going to kill me, too!"

Crocodile tears slid down Summer's cheeks as she stopped behind the detective. My cheek twitched at my sister's horrible acting skills. Maybe it was just me because I know her, but the detective seemed oblivious to the act.

Anderson gave her a proud nod and turned to face me with an expression of righteous indignation.

"Don't worry, sweetheart. You're safe now," he said. "And as for you. Prison's too good for you, you sick fuck."

Behind the detective, I saw Summer winking at me and raising the blade—which she had somehow kept hidden from the detective—above her head. She brought the pointy end down into the detective's back.

George Anderson yelped. The barrel of his gun kicked upward just as a shot fired. The ceiling splintered, and the detective was on the floor with Summer's knife going in and out of his back.

His coat was drenched in a mix of rain and blood. I lowered my hands because I deemed it safe enough to do so. Summer gave the detective another couple of stabs and then stood up, panting.

"Wait, isn't he that annoying cop from the TV?" she asked.

"Yup. The one and only," I said as I approached him.

The detective was still alive, moaning, the hand still on the gun but visibly loose and feeble. I kicked the gun out of his reach with ease, planted my foot on his shoulder, and pushed him on his back. His moaning momentarily became louder.

He raised both hands, intermittently glancing from Summer to me.

"Please..." he said.

The look of fear didn't suit him. I thought the only facial expression he was capable of making was the one he made when he visited me in the office—calm, stern, reticent. He didn't strike me as the kind of guy who ever lost his cool.

Or maybe he did.

The hate I saw on his face when he first barged into the cabin... I could see that same face at his home while he beat his wife with a belt. I put my hands in my pockets and looked at my sister. She was waiting for me to give the green light.

"What do you want to do?" she asked.

"Well, we can't let him go." I shrugged.

I looked up at her and the knife dangling in her hand. I came up with an idea in that moment.

"You know what? How about you take this one?" I asked.

Summer raised her eyebrows.

"Really?" she asked, a grin forming on her face.

It was the same kind of smile she'd display when we were kids and our parents promised to take us to Disneyland.

"Yeah. Finish him how you like. But next time, you're following my instructions. Got it?"

"You're the best, sis," Summer said as she brought the knife down on the screaming detective.

17

PORTLAND EXECUTIONER

It was a quiet night. I sat in the living room, mindlessly flicking through channels. Summer had been in the bathroom for the past forty minutes. She usually takes her time.

There used to be a time when I would find the bathroom door locked twice a day for over one hour each time. It was Summer going through a phase of taking long baths instead of showers. I found it annoying, especially when I needed to use the bathroom, but I never openly complained about it to her.

The weather report appeared on the TV. Snow. Yikes. Snow around this time of the year was horrible. It was never enough to cover the city in a beautiful blanket of white.

Instead, it would melt immediately upon touching the ground, and the ongoing traffic would make the melted snow dirty and spread it all over the streets so that both driving and walking were a pain in the ass.

Thank God it was Saturday tomorrow.

The door of the bathroom opened and out stepped Summer with one towel wrapped around her torso, the other around her hair.

"Hey, sis. Mind if I borrow your lipstick? I've been dying to try out that color with my new clothes," she said.

"Where are you going?" I raised an eyebrow.

She dismissively waved. "Don't worry. Not doing that tonight. Did you see what kind of weather we got? I hate winter."

"So, then what?" I asked.

"Girls' night out."

"Wow. Been a while since you've had one of those."

"Yeah. Wanna come with?"

"No!" I wrinkled my nose.

I suddenly became aware of the pajamas I was wearing. Just the thought of having to slither out of them, put on some night-out clothes, and actually step outside, away from the comfort of the warm apartment, made me feel sick.

"Suit yourself," Summer said as she strode back to the bathroom. "We're still on for tomorrow, though, right?" she shouted.

"Wait, what?"

"Tomorrow! You know? That CEO who sexually harassed his employees?"

"Aw, crap. That's tomorrow?"

"Uh-huh. But if you don't want to go, I can go alone."

Summer's words came out distorted as if she didn't properly close her mouth at certain consonants when speaking. *Probably putting her lipstick on*, I figured. *My lipstick.*

"No, no. I'll go. I need to show you the ropes anyway before we have another skateboard incident."

"It's not my fault he squirmed so much!"

"If you had done what I told you, he wouldn't have squirmed, to begin with."

"Okay, fine. We'll do it your way tomorrow."

I had started to feel a hankering for something sweet around that time. We had a blueberry pie in the freezer that had been sitting there for weeks now. I'd been saving it for my cheat meal day, but I felt so good eating healthy that I didn't want to ruin the streak.

It's amazing what happens to your body after you get rid of sugar. During the first few days, you crave it really bad, especially if you have a sweet tooth. Really, it's like an addiction, and nutrition experts even claim sugar has the addictive properties of cocaine.

Anyway, after you brave the first waves, it becomes easier. You wake up less lethargic. You have more energy for activities during the day. You're in a better mood. And most importantly, you start noticing a difference in your weight, appearance, and skin color.

This goes on for a while, but then you start craving sugar again after some time. It becomes stronger and stronger, and you wish you could have just one bite out of that chocolate cake sitting in the fridge.

But you can't because one bite will turn into ten, and before you know it, your diet streak will be over, and you'll convince yourself that one meal was just as okay as one whole day's menu, so you'll eat. Then you'll remember that it's the middle of the week, and you'll want to wait until Monday.

When Monday comes, a minor inconvenience would convince you that you deserved that dessert that you planned on skipping. And round and round it goes.

Not for me, though. I have really good discipline.

I have cheat meals once a week or whenever I kill someone. Taking a bath is no longer a part of my post-murder ritual. I also indulge in having a slice of cake or some ice cream.

I'd been really good with my diet, and it was Friday. So, why the heck not? Why shouldn't I have the blueberry pie now?

I took it out of the freezer and let it defrost a little bit. Summer had been buzzing between the bathroom and bedroom, wearing more pieces of clothes with each trip. Thirty minutes later, she was fully dressed, ready for girls' night out.

"Wow, you'll have a lot of guys flocking to you tonight," I said.

"I hope I find a nice one. You know, whenever I meet someone, I tell him that I'll kill him if he doesn't treat me nice. They always think I'm joking."

I laughed.

"Well, see ya," Summer waved and was out.

They grow up so fast, I thought as I watched her striding out of the apartment with confidence. I kind of missed the days when she was Little Red Riding Hood. But she hasn't been Red Riding Hood for a while now. It was just a clever disguise that she used to trick everyone around her.

Hell, *I* was the Red Riding Hood all along.

I changed the channel, and the news popped up. I was about to change the channel, but the headline at the bottom of the screen caught my attention.

PORTLAND EXECUTIONER STRIKES AGAIN.

The news showed the president talking about some negotiations while mini-news slid across the screen at the bottom. The Portland Executioner was all over the state nowadays.

People received the message the Executioner was trying to convey, and they took it upon themselves to bring justice to the country. The crime rate has gone down significantly because, wherever you were, there was always someone willing to put on the mask of the Portland Executioner and visit you at your home while you were peacefully sleeping.

Hell, there was even a convicted murderer who came up on the news a few days ago when he killed his cellmate and four other people (all of whom were rapists or pedophiles).

He was already on death row, and when asked why he did it, he simply said, "Because of the Portland Executioner." I opened Facebook on my phone and walked up to the counter. Of course, my newsfeed was flooded with the Executioner news.

As always, people were divided, but the majority supported what the Executioner stood for. It's always like that, isn't it? No matter what happens in the world, there are people who support the other side no matter how obviously wrong it is.

Sometimes, I think if we had aliens invade our planet with the intention to eradicate us, there would be activists fighting for extraterrestrials' rights.

The Executioner wasn't just on the news anymore. Executioner-themed merch like toys and T-shirts sold everywhere. Hashtags took over the internet. Cosplayers had photoshoots dressed as the butcher lady from the mural that represented the Portland Executioner, etc.

It wasn't just my legacy anymore. It was everyone's. And with so many people posing as me, the police were completely confused about the trail, which worked well in my favor because, not only did I not need to worry about getting caught, but I could also take it easy because I knew there were more vigilantes out there.

An article that said ANOTHER CHILD RAPIST DEAD THANKS TO THE EXECUTIONER popped on my news feed.

I smiled as I cut a slice of the blueberry pie.

THE END

Feel Free To Scream

FINAL NOTES

Thank you for reading my book. If you enjoyed it, I would appreciate it if you left a review on the **Amazon Product page**. Your reviews help small-time authors like me grow and allow us to continue expanding our careers and bring you – the readers – more stories like these.

Feel Free To Scream

MORE FROM THE AUTHOR

Some people can't take no for an answer.

AVAILABLE ON AMAZON
(FREE WITH KINDLE UNLIMITED)